I0589493

Creative Texts Publishers products are available at special discounts for bulk purchase for sale promotions, premiums, fund-raising, and educational needs. For details, write Creative Texts Publishers, PO Box 50, Barto, PA 19504

FRIGGIN ZOMBIES by N.C. REED
Copyright 2015 by N.C. REED
Cover design by Laura Roth

Published by Creative Texts Publishers
PO Box 50
Barto, PA 19504
www.creativetexts.com

Friggin Zombies is an absolute work of fiction. After all, there is no such thing as zombies, right? Any resemblance to actual names, persons, businesses, and incidents is strictly coincidental. Locations are used only in the general sense and do not represent the real place in actuality.

ISBN: 978-0-692-55364-0

Library of Congress Control Number: 2015954699

FRIGGIN'

ZOMBIES

(NO REALLY, IT'S ZOMBIES!)

This book is dedicated to my zombie-loving friends who will know who they are, including you Tara.

And of course to those who scour the internet in an attempt to know when the zombies are coming and what to do when they get here.

CHAPTER ONE

This is ridiculous. I mean seriously.

I work for years, since I was in high school for crap's sake, to be prepared for any emergency, anytime. I study, I train, I keep up with the news. I look for new products, I scour the web for suggestions about things I should always have on hand.

I took training courses. First aid, advanced life saving, volunteered for my local fire department and trained to fight fire, extricate people from crushed cars, whatever the situation called for. I took private, and *expensive*, training programs for almost every kind of scenario or event I could imagine, read about, or hear a rumor of.

Plague? Got it.

Nuclear, Biological or Chemical attack, by terrorists or in war, either one? Got that too.

Massive earthquake like that one in Japan that tore up the nuclear plant? Ready for it.

Horrendous hurricane that levels everything in its path? Even though I lived hundreds of miles inland, still prepared for it. Could work for tornado outbreaks too after all, right?

After all that time, sweat, money and even a little blood, what do I get? What great, earth changing event happens?

Zombies. The friggin' Zombie Apocalypse. George Romero style, I'm talking' about. Corpses walking the streets, fields, and creeping through the woods, hungry for human flesh.

Are you *kidding* me?

It started overseas apparently, though with the way that governments and corporations all over the world lie and hide information these days there's no real way to know exactly what happened. I sure as hell don't know, and to top it all off, things actually went down just about like it was a bad movie, or a good novel, or both.

First, there was a story on the news about a rare strain of rabies with a high mortality rate. They said it was not airborne, so there was no reason to panic, and there was my first mistake; I believed them. Remember I said I was ready for a plague? I should have went into plague mode right then, I guess, but hey, it's overseas, right? Africa or southern Europe, Asia, hell I don't remember, but it wasn't *here*, so no worries. Sure, it's something to keep an eye on, watch out for, but it's not a problem I should have to deal with.

Wrong.

The second warning, maybe three days later, was that this new 'rabies' had broken containment and was spreading. There were no reports of sickness in North or Central American so again, like a *dumb ass*, I ignored it. It was not near me, had nothing to do with me, something to watch for later on, if it gets worse, treatment options being developed, everything was under control, blah, blah, blah.

My ass.

The third warning, which I *finally* paid attention to, was a viral video showing what looked like a riot in some European city. Well, town, wasn't really a city, say about five, maybe six thousand people it looked like. Can't even remember the name of it. I think it was in Spain. Yeah, pretty sure it was Spain.

Anyway, the video was shaky since the guy or gal who was taking the video was understandably on the move while filming. You can see a stream of what, at least at first, looks like a bunch of really angry people, stumbling along causing havoc in the streets. Soccer team lost the cup or something? I almost clicked off, but for some reason, thank the Lord above, I kept watching. Call it morbid interest, boredom, I really don't know why, but I did.

At some point the video maker had to stop running for some reason. Maybe there was something in the way, I don't know. But for a few precious seconds the images were steady and clear. No problem seeing the action.

And there it was. The 'rioters' were stumbling all over the place, attacking anyone that got within their reach. I noticed that a few of them looked bloody, but that didn't ring a bell with me yet since, well, riots are violent and people get hurt.

FRIGGIN' ZOMBIES

Then as I'm watching three of the 'rioters' catch a woman with a baby in her arms in the middle of the street trying to run away. They literally fell onto her, and started. . .well, biting...*chewing* almost. The last thing you could see clearly just before the view went shaky again, was that two of the 'rioters' were missing large chunks of flesh themselves, a woman from her arm and a man from his shoulder. At first I didn't catch it, but when I studied the video later, frame by frame, it was apparent that both of those injuries were just about the right size for a bite wound.

A *human* bite wound.

The next thing I noticed, again going frame by frame, was the fact that the eyes of rioters were. . .well, empty looking. I mean, they still had eyes, but there was no one home, if you know what I mean. I admit it wasn't that great a shot but the look was clear enough to realize that I was looking at someone who wasn't with us anymore.

I remember my world tilting on its axis for a few minutes as realization came to me. At first it was just dull shock, you know?

Looking for a rational reason for things to look like this, be like this. It had to just be a symptom of the disease, right?

"Okay genius", my subconscious seemed to say, *"if it's a symptom of disease, is the 'riot' another symptom?"* I remember watching the whole thing again, in slow motion this time rather than frame-by-frame. This time I watched the so called rioters as they rambled along. There was no organization, no attempt at any kind of communication or co-ordination between them. It was just a group of. . .well, *zombies*...moving down the street in search of prey.

I admit it. As soon as the shock of what I had seen began to wear off, I panicked for a while. Firstly, I questioned everything that I had seen. Was I imagining it? Was there another explanation? Were all of the 'rioters' injured? Okay, *bit*? I watched the video again, not really wanting to but needing to clarify.

Slow motion helped with the shaky video quality and I enlarged it on my computer so I could get a better look. Every person in the crowd that I could get a decent look at was bloody. I couldn't always tell from where, but I could see that several of them had blood running down their chins. As if they had bitten someone and brought the blood, as the saying goes.

Finally, I leaned back in my chair, almost exhausted from simple stress of watching while my mind ran crazy with the idea that real live. . .er, *dead*, zombies were on the loose somewhere in Spain. I wasn't crazy. There were only two possible explanations.

One, this was a massive hoax. Some kind of movie footage, edited to look like a phone camcorder video of a real 'incident'. A giant prank, executed by a huge number of people in a small town where the entertainment value was pretty low. You know, boring weekend, few people get together to play a prank, it grows, and BAM, instant viral video with a town full of people drinking beer and congratulating themselves on fooling, scaring, and terrifying millions of people.

Two, there were zombies on the loose somewhere in Spain. Try as I might, I couldn't come up with another reason of any kind. Combining that with the news reports I had pretty much ignored for however many days, I decided that Option Two was going to be the winner.

Panic set in again almost at once. I wasn't prepared for a zombie apocalypse. I mean, sure, I was pretty well set for stores and supplies, but. . .I mean, if this worked anything like the movies and the zombie thing spread and came here where I was. . .

I'm sure anyone watching me would have seen the color drain from my face as I realized that the face of the *entire world* might be changing, right in front of me. My mind again went a little crazy, imagining being holed up somewhere, probably my house, surrounded by walking dead people who had only one desire—sinking their teeth into my flesh. I would be alone, surrounded, cut off, forever.

Forever.

Until I *died.*

FRIGGIN' ZOMBIES

At that point I decided my next step was to get a good stiff shot of bourbon and sit down in my seldom used recliner. It wasn't that there was nothing to be done. The fact was that my mind was overwhelmed by the scope of what *might* be coming, and the fact that it only might be coming was the first thing hurdle to overcome.

I couldn't afford to just quit my job and hole away from the world on the chance that a Zombie Apocalypse was coming. I mean, what if it got contained? Not only would I look like an idiot, I'd be out of a job which I liked and paid me well.

On the other hand, I couldn't just ignore the problem, either. What if it *wasn't* contained? What would I do then? How much did I have to do in order to be prepared to basically live out the rest of my life in my house? At that thought, I took a look around me.

My house was decent size for a single fella. Four bedrooms, one of which I used as a den/study/library/whatever. It had an attached garage, half of which I used as a small shop, two acres of land, give or take, enclosed by a sturdy four foot high chain link fence, and a medium size barn where I kept my mower, garden tools, outdoor toys, stuff like that. Like I said, for just me it was awesome.

But it would get awful small, awful fast if my whole world shrunk into just my little place of heaven. I started looking over my place in my mind's eye. I had a small garden plot which I ate from every year. I had a rain water collection system but no well. I could store water of course, but storage was roomy, expensive and let's face it...stale water sucks. And it runs out. I already had two large barrels of water for temporary storage, just over one hundred gallons, but I changed that out every three months.

One thing I *did* have was a thousand gallon cistern. It was sometimes a pain to keep clean and I had been meaning to clean it out and paint the walls with the stuff they use on swimming pools, but I had never gotten around to it.

That would have to change, I decided. I'd need to be able to use that cistern to store rain water if The End happened. I did already have a good filtration system in place, but I'd need to get some extras. I always kept one on hand but if The End happened, I wouldn't be able to get more. I would need more. At least, Lord willing I would need more. You know, if I didn't wind up on the Zombie buffet line.

I thought about my firearms. I had several, some just because I enjoyed shooting, but a few were simply survival arms. Things I had decided I might need in the event of a real disaster of some kind. I was also a re-loader, almost a necessity if you liked to shoot much, but I really didn't keep a lot of supplies on hand. It was just a hobby after all. I'd need to lay in more stuff of that nature.

I felt a headache coming on about then as I realized that despite what I had thought, I was not nearly as 'prepped' as I had imagined. Not for something like this. I got up and started looking for a notepad and pen. I was gonna need to make a list.

And I could pretty much kiss most of my savings good-bye, probably. I worried about that for about two minutes. If there was a real zombie apocalypse coming then my money would be worthless, anyway. And if there wasn't, then I'd just be really, *really* prepared for any future emergency.

As the magnitude of what might be happening began to really set in, I thought, just for a moment, what was the *point*? Would I want to live here alone struggling to stay alive for what might be *years*, if I was surrounded by walking death? It took only a minute for me to shake that thought off. I was a survivor. I was going to make it.

I took my seat again, leaning back, trying to think long term. I had some solar power. Of course it would never be enough to run my freezer and refrigerator, or my a/c either, when it comes to that. But, it would power my computer a few hours a day, it could keep my battery power tools charged, and it would power my television and DVD player, as well as my CD player. I would have some entertainment to break up the monotony.

But I would need books. I had plenty of books already, but for the most part they were books on preparedness skills, home improvement, gardening, and other DIY books. I would need some good books. Books I could read over and over again without losing interest. I decided that should go on the list.

I suddenly imagined myself growing old surrounded by zombies. Each year things getting harder and harder to manage, each year getting just a little slower, harder of hearing, eyesight fading. I added some dollar store type glasses to the list. No point in having books if I couldn't read 'em, right?

I was in pretty good health. A knee that tended to give me trouble once in a while from an old football injury, but otherwise I was in pretty good shape. I didn't take any kind of maintenance medications, but what about OTC stuff? What about a tetanus shot? I couldn't remember the last time I had gotten one. I put 'get a physical' on the list. I needed to see my doctor. Maybe I could talk her into some prescriptions for pain relievers and antibiotics, too. They'd fade in potency with age but be better than nothing.

Then I remembered a book on herbal medicine I had. I needed to look at that. Make sure I purchased the plants I'd need to make home remedies. First I'd have to make a list of what they were, and then hopefully find somewhere to get them, and then learn how to use them. Did they need to be dried? Mixed with something else? Did I have it?

My headache was getting worse as all this bombarded me. There was a lot to do and probably not much time. I sketched out a list of things to do tomorrow, including calling in sick. Since I was going to the doctor anyway, might as well take the day off. I could talk to the doc about what was happening in Europe. Maybe she was up to date on the latest since it was being broadcast as an illness.

But would she tell me? Maybe she wouldn't know anything but what was on the television. Was there some kind of warning system for doctors that broadcast super-secret medical information to them in secret code? For all I knew, there might be. And if there was, would she be allowed to share that information with anyone? I mean, without Men in Black showing up on her doorstep? Did MIBs do anything other than UFO's? I snorted at myself in ironic humor. I really didn't know crap, did I?

I decided another bourbon was in order. The list was getting longer, and my headache wasn't subsiding. I was going to have some kind of stroke before I had a chance to survive the zombie outbreak. The thought made me freeze.

What the hell would I do if something like that happened? I'd be alone, unable to care for myself. If I survived the stroke, or whatever, I'd just lay there and starve, or dehydrate, or whatever. Jeez, if it wasn't one thing it was another. What the hell was I going to do?

Finally I decided that there was nothing I *could* do. Going it alone wasn't going to work, and I knew no one that I trusted enough to take into my confidence on something like this. I wasn't really anti-social, don't get me wrong. I just wasn't much of a *socializer* and I never let on about my business much, personal or otherwise.

This needed sleep, and a fresh perspective. The bourbon was working on me pretty good now, and I decided it was time to sleep on the problem, and face it fresh in the morning.

Friggin' Zombies. Go figure, man

CHAPTER TWO

Well. After a good night's sleep. . .who am I kidding? I hardly slept a wink, tossing and turning most of the night worrying about zombies and shit.

Friggin' zombies.

Sounded just as insane in the daylight as it had the night before.

I got up early that next morning since I wasn't really sleeping anyway. If the Zompocalypse happened then I'd have plenty of time to sleep. Right? Or would I? Every movie or book I had ever read about zombies had them moaning all the time. That would get on a man's nerves, I figured. I stopped stressing long enough to add earplugs to my list. Wouldn't be no friggin zombie moaning keeping me awake. No sir.

Anyway, I called my doctor and was able to get a late afternoon appointment. That worked good for me since I had a lot of other crap to do. I called my job and coughed my way through a 'I'm sick and won't be in today' line, then got a shower. It was while I was in the shower that I realized that my cistern wasn't plumbed into the house. If the water went, then I'd need that solar shower rig I took camping once a year. Better make sure it's in good shape. I could always make one a new if I had to.

My list was growing longer by the minute it seemed. I got online and checked on solar power rigs. I could get a hundred eighty watts of power for about fifteen hundred, not counting batteries. I'd need batteries. I could always buy used car batteries if I had to, but batteries were something I didn't think I'd want to skimp on at the end of the world. Used batteries wouldn't last as long. What I really needed was deep cycle marine batteries.

I sighed. My savings were definitely toast. Ah well, like I'd said before, if things went south then my money would be worthless anyway. Might as well get some use out of it.

I needed to talk to an electrician maybe, and see if I could figure out a way to run a freezer. I had a generator, but that took fuel and I usually only kept five or ten gallons for it just in case we had power outage. The generator could actually run the house as long as it was wide open, but that would burn fuel like a California wildfire going through one of those cedar shingle neighborhoods. I'd never have enough. I could get some extra and use the generator in an emergency to charge the batteries, but using it to run the house was a no go. Just too impractical.

That meant a smoke house. I would need meat, and the only way to preserve it was to smoke it. How long would that last? Another item for the list. Pretty soon I'd look like Santa, with a list as tall as the Empire State Building. That made me wonder if the North Pole would have zombies? Maybe I should move to Alaska while I had the time.

I took about an hour to study the internet for news. Nothing new really, other than the standard 'virus continues to spread' crap. There were no new videos, and the one I'd seen the day before was gone by then, scrubbed completely from the web. That, more than anything else, convinced me there was a real problem and that I wasn't being paranoid. Which was enough to shake off the last tendrils of doubt and get my ass moving.

The Zombies were coming.

While I was online I decided to research alternative methods of keeping meat over long periods. First thing that popped up was freeze-dried foods and I almost did the V8 slap on my forehead. I had completely forgotten about stuff like that. I didn't have a good excuse, either, since I used that stuff camping. I punched up one of the more popular company's website, and started looking at what was available. I was worried that there wouldn't be much, but the site showed almost everything in stock.

And there it was. Fish or cut bait. Here was the chance to fix one of the big weaknesses I had in my preparedness for something like this. I sat back into my chair, considering my next move. I did that for almost thirty seconds before I was back to the keyboard, and punching in numbers. I noticed a toll-free number to call for orders, and on an impulse I decided to call the order in. I would be glad I had before it was over.

The woman who answered sounded a bit harried, but was still friendly.

"Busy day?" I asked her, trying to project a calm disinterest.

"Unreal," she replied. "Seems like everyone decided to order at once. We're selling out fast."

"Am I too late to get my order up?" I asked, forcing a laugh. "Lot of disappointed campers if I am," I added, laughing again. *Like what, me? worry? nah, not me!*

"No, you're in under the wire," she laughed in return. "All orders processed in the next three hours will ship no later than opening tomorrow, guaranteed. After that, though, I just don't know, to be honest. Now what can I get for you?"

I had a list and ran down it, careful to be calm and considerate. I offered my card information and made sure they had the proper delivery address. No work tomorrow looked like. Or the next day, either most likely.

The bill was high, but less than I'd expected. I printed off the receipt and stuck it into my desk with a big sigh of relief. That was one worry I could cross off my list. I'd need to make sure about some other stuff, like propane and what not, but food I had. Three years of it, on it's way in less than twenty-four hours. Sounded quick enough, but the clock was ticking in a big way.

I looked at my watch, and decided to set the countdown for seventy-two hours. I figured if things were going to get out of hand, it would be right around there if the spread continued like it had so far. I'd have to really be on the lookout, though.

I spent the next forty-five minutes going through my house, list in hand, writing notes on any and every thing that occurred to me while I was at it. It kept growing. By the time I was done with the house, then the grounds, my small shop, and my barn, I had three legal pages of list. That was a lot of list.

I decided to use my cards as long as I could, and save what cash and metals I had for what might come after. Cash was king until everyone figured out that it wasn't going to be worth squat if this got out of hand. And there was always the hope, back then, that it wouldn't.

I gathered up my stuff, more than I normally carried today, and headed into town. I lived only a couple miles out of a medium sized little town. One that would offer me everything I might need for what I feared was coming. Well, most everything, anyway.

Probably.

I spent the time between then and my doctor's appointment filling my trailer and then my cargo van with gear and supplies. I spent a good bit on groceries, even with all the other stuff I had coming. I bought plenty of beans, rice, flour and corn meal to stretch the canned stuff I had ordered. Anything to fight food fatigue, you know? Sugar, salt, and plenty of spices rounded off that list.

Next was new fuel tanks and fill them up. I hated to leave them in the trailer full up, but. . .well, I didn't know for sure that I'd get the chance to fill them once the shit

hit the fan. I bought five new cans and filled them. Tomorrow, I'd do the same thing again. After that, I'd have to see what happened.

Next was to the first of three gun stores I traded with on a regular basis. I got powder, primers and bullets, along with other odds and ends. I also picked up several (thousand) rounds of new ammunition in calibers for the guns I owned. Extra magazines for pistols and rifles that used them and parts and pieces for the weapons I owned. Buffers, springs, pins, that kind of thing. No sense in having a bunch of ammunition and not having anything to shoot it from, right?

Next was a hardware list of power tool batteries, hand tools, oil and grease, parts and supplies for chainsaw and mower, several lengths of chain, tape of all kinds, the list went on and on. I added several two-by-fours and three sheets of one inch plywood, just in case. Might need to build something, or board up my windows. I had shutters on my windows, actual working storm shutters in fact, but stuff breaks, you know? Better to have and not need and all that.

Finally I took a break, and went to lunch. I sat in the far corner of the Jack's restaurant, ordering myself both the double Big Jack cheeseburger and the ten piece chicken finger meals, plus a shake. They make good shakes with real Blue Belle ice cream. . .well, they used to anyway.

I hoarded my food and my lists in that corner, checking off all that I had managed to get done so far. A check of my watch showed that I still had about two-and-a-half hours until my appointment, so once I finished foundering myself on fast food and dairy I made the trip to a discount shoe place and picked up two new pairs of boots and two more of sneakers, along with two dozen pairs of socks. What? I get cold feet, okay?

Then it was off to a few last box stores for odds and ends, including duct tape. Man just can not have too much Duck Tape or Gorilla Glue. I can fix anything with those and a hammer, one way or another. People looked at me a little odd when I got to the check out with ten rolls of duct tape, ten more of electric tape, and six bottles of Gorilla Glue. Since there wasn't enough Duct Tape to suit me, I had scrounged around and located four rolls of Gorilla Tape. Good stuff, Gorilla Tape. I mean you know a gorilla will be stronger than a duck, right? Right.

After that, I checked again. My countdown was already down to sixty-six hours. Damn. That was quick. It was also time for me to head to the doctor's office.

Now, a few words about my doctor. She's *hot*. I mean like God Almighty, I break out into a sweat just thinking about her *hot*. And single. *Straight* and single. Nothing against those who play for the other team or anything, but I figure a good lesbian girl just won't show any interest in me, whereas with my straight, athletic, *lovely* doctor there was always that slim, last man on earth chance that she'd say 'yes' if I asked her out.

You know, once I worked up the courage to ask her out. Which, looking at my watch again, I needed to go ahead and do if I was going to. Well, might have waited too late for that. We'd see.

Anyway, I knew as soon as I pulled up to the clinic that I wasn't the only one who had the idea to see the doctor today. Up until now I had almost convinced myself that no one in my sleepy little area had noticed what was happening. Maybe they had and were just going about their own lists in a different order from me.

Sure enough, the waiting room was still jam-packed. I walked to the desk and spoke to the receptionists, signing in as I did so. She assured me it would be at least an hour before I heard my name called. I told her I had a few errands to run and she agreed that I had time, so long as I was back and inside by closing which was five pm. No problem, I assured her and departed again.

The only real errand I had was to visit a used book store in the middle of town but it kept me from sitting in a room full of potential sick people for over an hour. I spent the next forty-five minutes looking through shelf after shelf of used books, most in better shape that you might think. I selected about two dozen paperbacks and I think nine hard covers in the end. At the last minute I threw in some handy-man type books I saw on the way to the counter. There was a set of them, nine in all, from back in the day. Considering what might be coming, I could use them I figured. I paid for my new library and stored them behind the front seat of my van then headed back to Doctor Hottie's office.

Did I mention my doctor was flaming hot? I mean dear Lord how *did* you get all that in those jeans *hot*? Oh, I did? Sorry.

I still had to spend about twenty minutes sweating it out in the waiting room and germaphobe that I was turning into I had to use those handi-wipes that everyone was keeping at the door these days to clean the seat I was using. That drew some rather ugly looks from some of the people inside, especially the women, but having just watched one small child of about four clean his nose the way toddlers will, and then clean his hand on a chair when he was finished, I decided I would risk the ugly looks. If the world went the way I was terrified it might, most of these people might be zombie chow by the end of next week anyway, right? No point in worrying about running into them again, at Doctor Hottie's or anywhere else.

Sounds crass I guess. I don't mean it to be. What was I supposed to do? Announce to them 'oh, by the way? Zombies are on the loose in Spain and some other countries who's names I can't pronounce so you might want to stock up on ammo, edged weapons, and beef jerky?' Yeah, that would be a dandy way to get my work finished, spending the next seventy-two hours under mental observation.

No, thank you. But just know that it wasn't personal. I didn't have anything against any of them. Well, maybe that kid with snot on his hand, but even him I wouldn't have just left to a zombie. But do you really think his mom would have listened to me?

Yeah, me either.

Anyway, soon enough I was talking to the nurse, explaining that I had felt bad this morning, runny nose, slight fever, nausea, you know, the usual shit you tell the doctor when you want to be off sick for a few days. She nodded sympathetically, telling me 'it's going around', then left assuring me Doctor Hottie would be along shortly. And leaving me wondering what 'it' was and if I had 'it' now, after spending more than ten seconds in that germ infested waiting room.

That would be my luck though, you know? Make sure I'm prepared to ride out the Zompocolypse and then catch some respiratory disease and die just as the zombies started piling up. Shaking my head at the unfairness of it all, I used the sink in the exam room to wash my hands. Again.

I was still drying my hands when Doctor Calendar Girl came in. For once she wasn't drop dead gorgeous. Well, that's a lie since she's *always* drop dead gorgeous. But today she was out of sorts. Hair frazzled, face worn, clothes wrinkled. She did smile when she saw me though, making my heart and a few other things do a flip and flutter.

"Well, how's my favorite survivalist?" she grinned, looking at my papers.

"I need a tetanus shot," I told her without preamble. "I also need some antibiotics and painkillers if you can give them to me. Something with a decent shelf life. If I can get more than one script, that would be extremely cool as well." She had stopped reading and making notes about half way through my introductory speech, looking up at me with a frown.

"You know I don't do much pain meds," she said. "As for the others, what do you need all that for? The tetanus I understand, since I don't even have a note of when you might possibly have had one last. What's going on?"

Doctor Hottie wasn't stupid by any stretch of the imagination. I should admit here that I knew her from more than just seeing her as my doctor. She was a member of the gun club that I helped to run. Is this a great country or what? Good looking woman, doctor, *and* she was a shooter. Damn good one at that.

"I'm not sure anything is going on," I admitted finally. "I'm. . .covering my bases, that's all."

"Then what do you *think* is going on?" she pressed. Ah, Connie. Oh, that was her real name, Connie Kane. Cool name, huh? Makes an impression coming and going, does Connie. Know what I mean?

I stood looking at her for a minute and then took my tablet from my bag, setting it on the table. I looked at her, nodded at the tablet, and she rattled off the password to the clinic's WI-fi. Soon I was on line, and showed her as quickly as possible the news items I had marked. She read them efficiently, eyebrows raising as she looked at me.

"I know about this," she told me. "It's a virus, probably an offshoot of Avian. Precautions are being taken at all ports of entry. There are no reported cases anywhere in the state."

I said nothing, just punched up the video from Spain. I pushed the tablet over to her again and she made it clear by facial contortions she was humoring me. Probably for the rest as much as anything. That changed about two minutes into the video. Maybe sooner, since I was watching her face and not the clock.

Suddenly she looked up at me, eyes wide. I just rewound the vid, hit the slow-mo and punched play again. Connie watched it without comment. Once it was over, she took out her script pad and wrote what I asked for.

"What are you doing about this?" she asked, handing over the papers.

"Right now I'm just taking precautions. Food, water, shelter -"

"Ammo," she cut me off, and I nodded.

"And ammo. And parts and fuel and whatever I can think of in the next. . ." I checked my watch, "sixty-four hours and. . .thirty-one minutes."

"What? Why that amount of time?" she asked, surprised.

"I gave myself seventy-two hours to be as ready as possible. That was before dawn this morning. After that, it'll either be over and I'll be taking it day by day, or things will be fine and I'll be back at work. Much poorer than I started off today. I don't know which."

She was silent for two, maybe three full minutes. That's a long time for a woman, or a doctor, to be quiet. Finally she looked at me and I could see the wheels turning.

"You think this is real, don't you?" she asked, serious.

"I think it's possible, yes," I nodded. "And that video was scrubbed from the net this morning. No mention of it anywhere."

"Well, that's a bad omen," Connie said absently. "I live in an apartment building here in town," she said, looking straight at me. I waited for more, but then realized *she* was waiting. On me.

"I'm fortifying my place," I replied, once I figured out what she wanted to hear. "I've got about two acres of fenced land and an extra bedroom. If you want to order some freeze-dried food, here's the number. You better hurry, they're about to sell out." I wrote my address on the paper and gave it to her. "Are you sure you want to do this? I might be wrong."

"That video looked pretty real," she temporized and I knew then she knew more than she was letting on. That wasn't fair.

"What do you know, Doc?" I asked. "Time for secrets is over, if we're going to work together." She seemed to consider that for a minute, then nodded.

"Fair enough. Yes, I've heard odd stories, but. . .look, I worked for Doctors Without Borders for three years before establishing my practice. I know people who are still over seas and I met foreign doctors that I became good friends with. Yesterday I got a message that made almost no sense from a friend of mine in Portugal. I met her and her husband in Zaire and we've stayed in contact ever since. Her e-mail was rambling on and on about how wonderful things were and how their children were growing so tall and her husband was working over-time to make sure that the kids were well taken care off, that sort of thing."

"So?" I asked. "That's not really odd sounding, to me."

"They can't have children," Connie replied. "And they work in a government hospital on a straight salary. There's no such thing as over-time. She's trying to tell me something without telling me. Until now, I had no idea what it was. Now, maybe, I do."

"You think she's warning you that this is real and they may be compromised?" I asked.

"That's just exactly what I think," Connie nodded. "Look, I've known you longer than anyone else here in town. You know I can shoot and I'm a doctor. Maybe together we can make it if things really get that bad. You want a partner?"

Well hell *yeah* I want a gob-smackingly hot doctor who can shoot and probably cook better than I can and is smart to boot for a partner! What the hell kind of a dumb-ass question is that?

"That might work," I said carefully, trying to look reluctant. Connie almost smirked at me.

"Drake, I know that you watch my ass every time I walk away from you. You know you want me. With you, I mean," she added with a grin that said she knew *exactly* what I *really* wanted.

Busted.

"Well, when you put it that way," I sighed. "If I'm going to have a partner for the end of the world, I can't think of anyone I'd rather spend the Apocalypse with than you, Connie." She grinned ear-to-ear.

"That's more like it," she said firmly. "All right, this is my address," she scribbled on a piece of paper from her pocket. "I have four more patients and then I need to run by the hospital. Can you give me two. . .no, make it three hours, then come to my place? I'll have some of my stuff already packed by then, maybe."

"You want to move in tonight?" I asked, shocked.

"No point in waiting," she shrugged. "My roommate is out of town, but if she gets back before the shit hits the fan can she come to? She really won't have anywhere else to go."

"Can she shoot?" I asked.

"She can, though I don't know how well. She's a good cook, I do know that."

"Well, all right I guess," I grinned. "Every guy I know will think I'm the luckiest SOB alive, this gets out," I laughed.

"And you just might be," Connie shot back at me with a malicious looking leer. "Better be on your P's and Q's buddy. Now, I have to go. Your scripts are printing up. Please, just in case this isn't the end of the world, pay cash for one of them, okay?"

"For both," I nodded. "I need a doctor's excuse for work, to," I added. "One that puts me off through next Monday or a little longer even. You can say I've got whatever crud that waiting room was full of." I gave her the fax number for my office. She frowned, tapping on her computer some more.

"They're going to give you a cocktail to kill anything you might have picked up here today," she told me. "Can't have you sick when the zombies roll in after all."

"You don't really think that will happen, do you?" I asked. I guess, maybe, I wanted someone smart to tell me that 'no, this isn't what it looks like.' Connie didn't oblige.

"Until you showed me that video I was concerned, but nothing else. Now? I've skipped worried and moved right on to 'afraid'. There's only two levels above that," she said.

"What are they?" I had to ask. I mean, I *had* to. You would have to.

"Bugging out and scared shit-less," she told me without missing a beat. "And I'm pretty much bugging out. Now, go and make room in your trailer, or unload, or whatever. I'll see you in a couple hours. I have a phone call to make and then patients to see." She held up the number I had given her for the freeze-dried food company. I nodded and waited for the nurse to bring my shots.

Of course. Zombies on the inbound and I get a big fat needle in both sides of my ass.

Friggin' zombies.

CHAPTER THREE

I gotta admit, I left the doctor's office feeling pretty good. Well, other than a knot beginning to swell on each ass cheek that is. Damn shots.

But *come on*. What guy *doesn't* dream of spending the end of the world with a hot as hell girl? Not me, I can tell you that much. Connie was as beautiful as she was smart and I knew for a fact that she could shoot damn near as well as I could. Despite the whole 'end-of-the-world' thing that was going on, things were definitely looking up as far as I was concerned.

I figured I had to stop day dreaming though and get some work done. I made a quick coughing call to my job, assuring them that I was almost dead with some kind of virus that I couldn't pronounce, had seen the doctor and been given a shot and some meds, and Lord Willing would be back sometime next week, hopefully Monday. I threw in a warning about 'it' going around, and hung up. I know, I know. Should have warned my co-workers. How, though? 'Hey guys, the zombies are coming?' Yeah, that would have gone over real well.

Anyway, I went to two different drugstores and left my prescriptions. While I was waiting for them to be filled I ran home and unloaded the trailer. Took a bit longer than I'd thought it would, and by the time it was finished I was winded. Still, things were looking better. Right?

With the trailer and the van unloaded, I locked my place down tight again and headed back to town. I had cut it pretty close but managed to make both pharmacies before closing, paying cash for my medicines. I had used pharmacies I didn't normally go to, since my regular pharmacy had my insurance information. While I was there, I picked up a buggy full of OTC meds and some stuff to add to my first-aid kit. And I got several gallons of bleach. Bleach kills any germ, right?

On a whim, literally at the last second, I got three boxes of condoms. What? Man can dream, can't he? Besides, there's no harm in being prepared.

With that done, I checked my watch. Sixty-two hours, fifteen minutes. Shit, where was the time going? I still had over an hour before I was supposed to meet Connie so I took out my lists and perused them again in the Walgreens' parking lot. Got that, got that, need that, *definitely* need that, and so on. I ran back to the Lowe's and bought four more gas cans, then headed to fill them up. Another twenty gallons of gas. I was careful to make sure all the tanks were treated. I also filled up the tanks on my van, adding stabilizer to them both. If I wanted to move once things went to hell I'd need gas, right? Plus, I could always siphon gas from the van to run the generator in an emergency. Smart huh? Thank you.

Once all that was done it was getting time to head for Connie's. If I was early then I could help her pack I figured. And I was getting hungry. Once we had her stuff loaded I wanted to get something to eat.

Connie's apartment was in a pretty nice place, with a gate and a wall. If the other residents had been on board it would probably have been a good place to hole up. But people, being people, were hard to predict. It was better to limit yourself to a few people that you knew you could trust and count on, right? I didn't know Connie's roommate, but I had trusted Connie to take care of my health for years, so I figured I was technically already trusting her with my life. Right? How was this really any different?

She apparently had been watching for me. As I pulled in she was waving to me from the door of a ground floor apartment. She'd also been busy. I could see tubs and suitcases sitting inside her door.

"Just in time," she smiled tiredly as I got out. "I'm about ready to go. Can you help me?"

Of *course* I could. In all kinds of ways. I shook my head at that. *Concentrate Drake. Concentrate.*

"That's why I'm here a little early," I managed to nod seriously. "What's first?"

It took about twenty minutes to get her things completely loaded. There were gun cases, ammo boxes and several tubs of emergency gear along with the suitcases and other tubs with her personal stuff. It was obvious that she was leaving a lot here, but then this might be temporary. We could always come back for the rest of her stuff if we needed to.

Well, probably.

Once we were done Connie leaned tiredly on the trailer, catching her breath.

"I'm hungry and exhausted," she said flatly. I nodded.

"Been a long day for me too," I agreed. "I thought we could grab a bite to eat first and then head to my place. You can unpack what you need for tonight and I'll get the rest later tonight or tomorrow. I assume you're working tomorrow?" She nodded.

"I've canceled all my appointments after Wednesday for next week. Rescheduled them for the week after. If there's still anyone to treat after that then I'll play it by ear. Eating sounds good to me. My treat," she smiled.

"That's not how I imagined our first date going," I laughed, only half joking. She laughed back, but was smiling.

"Don't worry about it," she pushed me slightly. "You can make it up to me later. If there is a later."

We headed to a small restaurant just outside of town, a nice little steak house that was locally owned. Probably one of the best places for beef anywhere. Well, it used to be anyway.

We had a good meal. By some kind of silent agreement neither of us mentioned the worries that had brought us together. There would be plenty of time for that, assuming we didn't get eaten. *If* anything actually happened.

Connie was a good conversationalist even tired, and I enjoyed the meal and the talk a good deal. Occasionally I found myself drifting away from the conversation, wishing I had asked her out a long time ago. I had no real excuse other than the fact that I was sort of anti-social, and she was painfully good looking, and what would she want with a guy like me anyway, and so on. You know, the usual.

Once we were finished we headed home.

I would imagine that her worst moment was right before we walked inside my house. When we first arrived she had given my place a once-over, nodding in apparent approval. It was an older home, one I had remodeled after I bought it. Solid timbers, old fashioned framing, a real house built in a time when stuff was made to last. I had spruced it up a good bit, but the guts of the place were still as solid as when it was first built.

I opened the garage door and bowed slightly, waving her inside. She stepped in, cautious at first and I decided that her good sense was finally kicking in. Why had she decided to come here, what was she thinking, how well did she really know this guy, you know; all that kind of stuff. I said nothing, following her inside with the suitcase she'd wanted for tonight.

She made it about five, maybe six steps inside before she stopped short, looking around her with surprise evident on her face.

What can I say? I like my comfort. Yes, I enjoyed the outdoors. Hunting, camping, off-roading, all that kind of thing. But I didn't want to *live* like that.

My house was pretty nice, especially considering I was a bachelor I suppose. It was clean, well furnished, and roomy. She looked back at me finally, eyebrows raised.

"What?" I asked, though I pretty much knew what was going through her mind.

"I'm at a loss for words," Connie admitted. "I admit I was a little apprehensive, but. . .damn, Drake, this is *nice*."

"Thank you," I nodded, grinning a bit. "I've had this place a while and I never seem to stop working on it, to be honest. Glad you like it."

"I might have visited you sooner if I had known how nice this place was," she told me, eyebrows raised. Once more my heart, and other pieces of my anatomy, fluttered.

"Well, happens this is all just a great big misunderstanding, feel free to come and visit anytime," I told her, more to cover my sudden, ah, fluttering, than anything else.

"I'll do that," she promised and the fluttering reached a new height.

"Here, let me show you to your room," I said, managing not to stammer. I led her through the dining room and down the hallway to the bedroom that I kept set-up for visitors. Thankfully it was very nice, and it had it's own bathroom, too. She whistled softly as I turned on the light and motioned for her to enter.

"Wow, Drake, you just keep impressing a girl, don't you?"

"If I had even dreamed you would be impressed I would have shown you an album of this place at least two years ago," I told her truthfully. Damn it, she *had* to know the effect she was having on me. Hell, the effect she would have on *any* red-blooded American male who wasn't confused about his sexuality. I decided this was going to be a lot harder than I had first imagined. *Damn* it, I meant *more difficult.*

"Well, I'm going to get a shower and hit the bed," she said suddenly. "It occurs to me that I'll need a ride into town in the morning since I rode here with you," she added. "Sorry."

"I'll be up before dawn anyway," I shrugged. "Lots still to do, and not much time to get it done. By the way, did you get your food ordered?"

"Yes, and apparently just in time," she nodded. "The operator that took my order told me that they were suspending all orders after closing today. My order is supposed to ship tomorrow and be delivered here."

"Good deal," I told her, relieved. "I'll try and get all my other running finished after I drop you off in the morning. Once that's done I'll work on making sure this place is tight, so I'll be here when the delivery gets here. Make sure and get me a list of what you ordered." I pointed to the small chest next to the bathroom door.

"Towels, bath-rags, extra blankets and what have you," I told her. "There's some soap and shampoo already in the shower if you need them. There's an alarm clock on the night stand. If you need anything let me know. Good night."

"Night, Drake," she smiled tiredly. "And Drake?" her voice caught me at the door. I turned.

"Thank you."

"Totally my pleasure," I smiled, telling the absolute truth. "Sleep well."

I sure as hell wouldn't. This was not how I fantasized getting Connie Kane under my roof or into my bed. Hey, that bed she was going to sleep in was *mine*, so technically I could say that.

I walked back to my study muttering under my breath. Not really at anything, just. . .well, come on, man. My absolute dream girl was in the shower in my spare bedroom right now and I was going to surf the net looking for news about zombies.

How screwed up is that? Right?

Forcing the image of my unbelievably hot doctor slash roommate in my shower lathered up and wet (*not helping, not helping, not helping*) I fired up my computer and started looking at news stories. Several of the original stories I had keyed on had been updated, and I faithfully read them all, saving them to my hard drive in case they disappeared overnight.

There was still no official panic, but the stories were beginning to take on a more concerned tone. For some of the reporters it seemed this was no longer merely a story. Maybe some of them had loved ones who had been affected, or perhaps they had learned the truth, either from their own experiences or from someone else. Either way, those reports had a more urgent feel to them.

One story in particular got my attention that night. It seemed that more than one small European town was experiencing power outages that somehow prevented communications outside of town. No phone or radio contact of any kind for the last twenty-four hours. Conveniently, each one of these towns had also had the bad luck to suffer damaged bridges or rock slides or some other minor catastrophe that prevented travel to and from the affected region. As Yoda might have said, *'Is strong with the bullshit, this one is'.*

Well, he might not have said it but I would have, and did. One, maybe two towns, sure. Stuff happens and that's a fact of life anywhere in the world. But when you have more than a dozen places, some of them widely separated from any of the others, all suffering from the same problems at the same time? Give me a break. Who's that stupid?

All right, all right. I know there are plenty of people who are that stupid. Well, were that stupid anyway, but I'm getting ahead of myself. Bottom line was, this was looking more and more real to me. Even if it wasn't some kind of zombie thing, clearly something was wrong in Denmark. And Spain. And Belgium and. . .well, you see what I'm saying. Someone in power was trying desperately to cover it up, but there was only so long you could keep something like this a secret. From the looks of these reports, it was clear that time was drawing to a close.

Another thing that was clear, at least to me, was that the problem, *whatever* it might be, was getting worse. Or at least spreading and doing it quick. I checked my watch. Fifty-seven hours, nineteen minutes.

I sat back, letting go of a long breath. My self-imposed time limit was running out in just as big a rush. I took out my lists again and started checking them over, making sure that I marked off everything I'd already accomplished. It was still depressingly long.

On the bright side, I wasn't going to be alone it looked like. Despite my hots for Connie, I admitted that her presence was comforting for other reasons. Sure, her being a doctor was a definite plus, but. . .considering my fears the night before, just having someone else around should things go south gave me a pretty good feeling. Of course, the fact that it was Connie made it a lot *better* feeling. I'd be lying if I said otherwise. But you get my point.

With my lists updated I decided to hit the shower and go to bed myself. I would need to be hard at it by sunrise, getting the trailer unhooked and the van unloaded. If I could do all that before heading to town, then I wouldn't have to come back to do it once I dropped Connie off.

Although I didn't think I'd sleep much, considering my company and all, once I'd stood under the hot water a while and then toweled off I hit the bed and went straight to sleep. Tomorrow's worries would wait for tomorrow to get here.

I hoped.

CHAPTER FOUR

By dawn I was awake and ready to go. Today I decided to abandon any hint of stealth, and strapped my gun on my belt to start with, along with an extra mag and some other accessories. I had too much to do and too little time to get it done to worry about scaring or offending anyone. Besides, I had a permit and I was on my own property.

I moved the trailer off to the side of the driveway, doors facing toward the garage to make it easier to unload later. The van didn't have a lot left in it since I'd unloaded it the night before and Connie hadn't left much inside. It was the work of only a few minutes to clear out the van and less than an hour to get the trailer. It was nowhere near as loaded as it had been when I'd brought my first load of stuff in. Once that was done I stood outside for a minute, thinking.

The van was my work vehicle but it was pretty handy for most other things, too. Still, if things really did turn all end-of-the-world on me, I'd need more than the van maybe. I'd need Big Baby. Realizing that I hadn't thought far enough ahead, I started for the barn.

Now Big Baby is. . .well, my baby. I mentioned I liked off-roading, remember? Well, I did that with Big Baby. I also took her camping, fishing, hunting, basically anywhere I could justify taking a 1972 K5 Blazer with a 454 cubic inch engine that was cranking right at four hundred horse power, a four speed heavy duty. . .well, you get the idea. Big Baby is a bad ass old girl. Four extra inches of lift to accommodate the oversize tires, heavy brush bumper that doubled as a water tank and air tank, roll bar with. . .I'm doing it again. Sorry. Thing is, Big Baby is my pride and joy. She's been re-built from fender to fender and bumper to bumper. If I could figure a way to get it on there, Big Baby's got it.

She also drinks gas like an elephant drinks water. To compensate she had twin oversize fuel tanks and a third tank beneath the bed liner. Their combined capacity gave me about eight hundred miles range without refueling. That may not sound like a lot, but thing is? That eight hundred miles could be over the worst ground in the area and I'd still be able to get there. As Fremont said, a man moves when he wants or he doesn't move at all. Well, Richard Chamberlain said it in a movie where he *played* Fremont anyway. So there.

Regardless of who said it, I liked to be able to move, come whatever. And Big Baby made sure I could move.

I checked all the fluid levels first, making sure she was ready to rock. I hadn't run her in a good while, and I was particular about that. I had too much time and money invested to let something silly or stupid mess her up. She was a little sluggish to start, but that was normal when she hadn't been run in a while. I let her idle for a few minutes and soon enough she was ready to go. I pulled out of the barn, stopping long enough to close the door again, then pulled around front.

Connie was in the kitchen when I went inside, already done up for another day as

Doctor Hottie. And damn she was hot. I mean great balls of fire get the water hose *hot*. I've said that before, haven't I? Sorry. Anyway, she smiled at me when I walked inside.

"Morning."

"Morning," I replied, getting my EDC bag. I looked through it briefly out of habit and then went to the closet and got my three day bag to put in the Blazer. I had decided it was just stupid to keep using the van if I had to be in town. I might really need to get home no matter what, and Big Baby would make sure I did. No matter what.

"You about ready to head in?" I asked, and Connie nodded.

"Can we stop somewhere and get breakfast?" she asked.

"Sounds like a plan," I nodded, and looked at my watch. Forty-seven hours and ten minutes left. Today was Thursday. The food we'd ordered might get here on Friday, or Saturday. I had paid extra to make sure mine was here in seventy-two hours and Connie had done the same. It was an extra expense, but. . .I figured if I didn't have it by then, I might not get it. If I didn't need it, then I'd just be poorer. A lot poorer. But I could always eat the stuff.

"I usually cook but I've been busy this morning," I told my new roommate. "What time do you have to be at your office?"

"By eight fifteen," she replied, looking at her own watch. "Plenty of time to get a bite and pick up my car. If we start now," she added, looking up at me.

"We're good," I nodded. "I already unloaded everything."

"I saw my stuff in the living room," she nodded. "I'll get it squared away tonight when I get back." I shrugged that off.

"Leave it there, or in the spare room if you want, until we see what happens. You may not have to unpack everything." I opened the door, holding it open for her. No sense in wasting a good opportunity by not being a gentleman, you know? Bad, Drake. Very bad. She smirked as she walked by. Busted again. Still made me smile.

She made it about two steps outside before jerking to a stop. I reached for my pistol but then I realized that she had just noticed Big Baby.

"What in the hell is that?" she asked, and the little tone of awe and surprise made me smile just a little.

"That is Big Baby," I informed her grandly. "She will make sure we can get around, no matter what happens. I'm taking her in this morning for an oil change and to fill up her tanks."

"Tanks?" Connie asked, moving again. "Plural?"

"Well, she burns a lot of gas," I shrugged. "So, yeah. Three tanks."

"How much does it cost you to fill this monster up?" she wanted to know, using the hand strap and the step ladder to get inside.

"Nowadays, around two hundred dollars, give or take," I answered. "It's not like I drive it much, though. Like I said, Big Baby's here in case of emergency. If things are turning bad, we can get around a lot easier than using the van or your car."

"And run over anything that doesn't move aside," Connie added. Maybe a bit tart, I thought.

"Now you're getting it!" I enthused, to which she replied with a snort.

We made it to town in good order and got us some breakfast. I dropped Connie at her apartment to get her car, where she was glad to see her roommate's car.

"I need to go and talk to her," Connie said, opening the door. "I don't have much time, but she needs to know what might be happening." She stopped and looked back over her shoulder at me. "Want to meet her?"

"Sure," I shrugged. I had time. And I honestly would have done pretty much anything she asked me to. What can I say?

Connie's roommate was named Rita. Rita Thomas. Redhead, freckles, cute. Nothing like Connie, but not in any way unattractive.

Rita scoffed at Connie at first, but Connie kept on hammering at her with facts, using my tablet and her own laptop to show Rita the business. In ten minutes, Rita's tune had changed completely.

"Got room for me too?" she asked, looking at me hopefully. She seemed like one of those people who are just naturally bubbly. I hated that in a person, especially early in the morning. But. . .any friend of Doctor Hottie and all that, right? Right.

"Yes," I told her. "Pack what you need to take with you, and I'll come back by and pick you up if you want. Or you can follow me out there," I added. "Either way."

"I'll need my car," Rita said thoughtfully. "I'll have work to do if this doesn't happen. You know it sounds crazy, right?" she looked at me doubtfully.

"I do," was all I said.

"Well, no sense takin' chances, I always say," she bubbled again. Ugh. Too early for that, even if the world was ending. "I'll get to work. Luckily I got the weekend off, so I'm good. It's my long weekend, since I was on call yesterday. I'm a home health care nurse," she added. Bubbly. Again. I shot a glance at Connie, who was hiding a grin. Almost an apologetic grin, I noticed. When

Rita turned to get a pen, Connie mouthed 'sorry' to me behind her friend's back. I just waved it off. If it got me in good with my goddess of medicine, then I'd make do. Bubbly or not.

"Here's my number!" Rita grinned, handing over a business card with her cell phone added to the back. "Give me a call when you head this way and I'll be waiting."

"Oh-kay," I sort of drug it out, and I swear Connie snickered just a little. It's really lucky for her she's my dream woman, or I'd have been very put out by that. A little. Some. Okay, you got me. I probably would have let a bear crap on me if it made Connie Kane look at me favorably. Know what I mean?

Anyway, I left Bubbly Red Rita to pack and headed for Chuck's garage. Chuck was a buddy. We road trails together some, and he had done a lot of work on Baby for me. Anytime it was something outside my skill set, I took it to Chuck.

Chuck happened to be free when I drove up and went right to work on Baby's fluid and filter check. We talked about odd and end stuff while he checked her over. He didn't mention the stuff in Europe and I didn't bring it up either. I liked Chuck, I really did. But he was straight red-neck. If I had told him he would have laughed me out of his garage, and by sundown the entire city would have thought I was nutty as a fruitcake. That was a complication I didn't need. Just did. Not. Need. So when Chuck was done, I paid him, gave him a little extra for beer since I wouldn't be out this weekend, and said good-bye.

Haven't seen Chuck since, I'm sorry to say. He was a pretty good guy. Thinking about all this makes me feel bad once in a while. I mean, I know that no one would have listened, you know? I could have yelled it from the courthouse steps and no one would have cared other than I might be disturbing them with the noise. So what do I have to feel guilty about?

Technically nothing. Nice word, technically. Means 'according to the rules, by letter of the law rather than spirit', and about a half-dozen other things all designed to make people who didn't do 'the right thing' feel better about themselves.

But seriously, what could I do? I wasn't even sure that 'it' was going to happen. I just had a really bad feeling based on a few minutes of amateur video that was no longer on the web, a few odd news stories that seemed to be falling into a predictable pattern, and a healthy dose of fear. No proof to show anyone and no way to substantiate a single thing I thought was going to happen.

What would you have done if someone had come up to you and said, 'H*ey, man. Like, I don't wanna start a panic or nothin' but. . .zombies are real, dude, and they're coming!'* Right. You'd have laughed right in their face, and told 'em to stop screwing' with ya.

Or called the cops. Either way.

It's easy to step back and tell yourself, *'Hey, they can look for things just like I can. If they aren't ready, it's their problem'.* Sounds good up to a point and it even makes sense. When did it become my obligation to do the watching and digging and looking for everyone else? I could have stayed at home drinking beer. . .well, I had stayed at home and drunk beer, but not to excess, all right? I was doing research.

I was watching news reports, videos, anything I could find that would tell me what was going on. If I can spend the time to keep up on stuff I need to know, so can other people. Problem is, most everyone depends on the 'goobermint' to tell them what's wrong and what to do about it. I mean, let's face it; the people in Dee Sea can't do the job they were sent there for in the first place, and you want to depend on them to give you timely information about a problem that could bring about a zombie apocalypse and perhaps the end-of-the-world?

Nah. That's too much trust to place in the hands of self-centered, self-important morons. I'll take care of myself, thanks.

Look, all I'm saying is that there was nothing I could have done any differently about folks like Chuck. They wouldn't have believed me. Would have ridiculed me and probably tried to have me arrested for observation. That's a real thing, you know. And I didn't have time for that. So, do I jeopardize my own safety and survival trying to help people who would just turn things around on me?

Well, I didn't. So sue me.

Anyway. . .with all that done I ran by the Lowe's one last time, picking up five more gas cans. Last five they had, in fact. I filled them and Big Baby, adding fuel stabilizer all around. The bill was something else for something like ninety gallons of gas. If it hadn't been for the end-of-the-world thing, there's no way I would have been spending that kind of money. Later on I'd be glad I did, but at the time it was just a throw of the dice.

I took a look at my well worn lists and realized that except for a few little odd and ends I was done. I picked up six new deep cycle marine batteries for the new PV cells I had gotten the day before. Another hefty chuck of money, but a good investment. Case of motor oil for Baby and at least one bottle of every fluid she needed. More fuel treatment, just in case. By the time I left the parts house, the manager was inviting me to his son's graduation from college. You know, since I was paying for it and everything.

Finally I couldn't put it off any longer. I pulled out my cell and called Bubbly Red Rita and listened as she bubbled to me that she was ready to go. Sighing in regret for the weakness I felt any time I was in Connie Kane's presence, I drove back to their apartment. Rita was ready all right. With what looked like everything she owned, ever.

"What the hell?" I asked, looking around the crowded living room. "Connie didn't have near this much, and you don't have a single gun case in the bunch! You can't possibly need all this stuff!"

"Well, I had to get my grandmother's dishes, and my Aunt Mary's bowl and picture and wash stand, it's antique you know, and then I can't leave my photos behind, and I've got. . . ." She droned on and on, just one long, never ending, migraine inducing sentence. I seriously thought about putting two in her head and driving away. If I hadn't been absolutely positive that it would have ended any chance I had of making it with Doctor Hottie, I would have.

Well, I would have left her anyway.

"Look, you can't take all this shit," I settled for saying instead. "Didn't Connie tell you just the essentials? Clothes, weapons, food, personals. Books and stuff are cool, but. . .you won't need your grandmother's dishes if this happens. And if it doesn't you'll be back here in a few days at most. Now you need to go through all this and decide what *you've got to have*, and that's all that's making the trip! I don't have room for all this stuff in my truck anyway," I finished.

"Oh, well, I figured we'd just make two trips!" Bubbly, bubbly, bubbly. So very easy. Just a quick draw, double tap, close the door. . . .

"I'm not making two trips," I managed to reply calmly. "I have other stuff that needs doing today and I also need to be around the house since we're expecting a delivery. Two of them in fact. I'm making one trip and not planning on another one. I'm certainly not burning ten bucks worth of gas to come and get a wash stand, antique or not. Period."

I swear, she looked like she was going to cry. Her bottom lip even trembled a bit. At this point, I admit it. I was starting to think that even my beautiful doctor was not worth this. And I assure you that Connie Kane was a woman I would have done damn near anything I was capable of to make a good impression on.

"But I need my things," she almost moaned. "I can't leave them!"

"Yes, you can," I assured her. "Look, we won't have room for all of this stuff anyway, once we've got everything else inside the house. You've got to prioritize, Rita. Clothes, toiletries, food, weapons, things like that. Things you will need to *survive* if all this comes to pass, understand? Your grandma's dishes and that other stuff will not help you when the shit hits the fan. And if it doesn't then you'll be back here surrounded by your things in a few days." I paused, frustrated. I could tell by the look on her face that Rita wasn't getting it. And wasn't going to give in.

"Look around you," I tried another track. "See all the stuff Connie left? She gets it. She only brought what she'll need if everything goes to hell in a grocery basket. You want pictures, bring a picture album with the most important ones. That's all you really need. You don't need dishes, you don't need bowls and pictures, you don't need *dolls*," I pointed to the pile of dolls she had ready to go.

I mean, come *on*. The world is friggin' ending and she's packing *dolls*? Are you *shitting me*?

"That's the way it has to be," I told her flatly, crossing my arms in front of me. I was through at that point. She either got it, or she didn't. I was suddenly very sorry that I had agreed to let Bubbly Red Rita come along. And that meant I might end up being sorry I'd asked the doctor, too.

What was I thinking? That's what ran through my mind for a split second. I could make it on my own. If I was being drug down by the Rita's of the world then I'd end up at the bottom of the food chain, no doubt about it. I wasn't going to let that happen. Damned if I was after all that work to try and get prepared for this.

"But. . .but my things!" Rita wailed, tears coming to her eyes. I shook my head and turned for the door.

"I need to be home soon," I said over my shoulder. "I'm sorry you can't live in the real world with the rest of us, Rita, but I don't have the time to baby you either. You're welcome to come along but there's a limit, and this," I waved my arm around to cover all that. . .*shit*, "is beyond it. Pare it down or you're on your own."

"But Connie said I could come!"

And there it was. I had made a huge mistake and I probably couldn't undo it. I turned to look at her.

"I didn't say you couldn't come," I told her flatly. "I said you can't bring everything you own. There isn't room, there isn't time. Leave what you don't need to survive here. If things don't go crazy, then it'll save you having to move it all back. If they do go nuts, you won't need them to get by." I stood there looking at her. She tried the trembling lip again, but there was no way that was working on me. Tears either. Threats would be ne. . .

"I'll call Connie!" Rita all but screamed. That was the last straw for me, thanks.

"Go ahead and give her a call," I told her, turning again. "I'm sure she'll be glad to come back and hide here with you instead of staying where she's safe and comfortable. See ya around, Rita. Nice meeting' ya." Okay, that part was a lie, but even angry there's no reason we can't be civil, right? Common courtesy.

I half expected to get a call from Connie on the way home, but it never came. I'd see what she had to say about it later, I guessed. For now, I had work to do.

*****

I had just finished walking the fence making sure it was in good repair when Connie pulled into the drive followed by another car driven by, you guessed it, Rita. It only took one look to see that she was mad. A sudden irrational need to slap her upside the head overtook me and it was all

73

I could do to fight it off. I had managed not to be mad about her scene earlier in the day but for some reason her pulling into my yard with that pissed off look set me right off.

Connie got out of her car and headed straight toward me. I braced myself, because I was not going to lose control of my home. Not even for her.

"I'm sorry," she said when she got closer. I don't know what I had expected, but that wasn't on the list. "I swear, I had no idea she was so stupid. I really though she had a clue, Drake."

"Is she straightened out now?" I asked, managing not to sound pissed off. I mean, hey, if Connie wasn't mad, then I wasn't mad, right? See how quick I can re-prioritize? I'm flexible that way. It's a gift.

"She only brought the essentials," Connie nodded. "She's still sulking, but I made her see the sense in it. Honestly, if we hadn't already told her, I'd have left her," she sighed. I took a long, adoring look at my absolute favorite doctor in the whole world at that. Which she promptly misunderstood.

"I shouldn't have said that," she half apologized. "Sorry."

"What? Oh, no, no. I. . .it just tickled me to hear you say that. The fact that she was your friend probably kept me from just shooting her, to be honest. Her voice may be the second most annoying sound I've ever heard in my life."

"What in the name of all the world is the first?" Connie asked with a laugh.

"Fingernails on the chalk board," I told her, and she shivered. Yeah, like you just did when I mentioned it. I know you did it. We all do. Well trust me, Bubbly Red Rita was almost just as bad. Seriously.

I watched for thirty minutes as the angry woman unpacked her car without asking for my help, shooting me an ugly glance every time she walked by. I refused to help unless she asked. I know, I know, it's petty. I'm shallow that way.

And it felt good, too.

She got the third bedroom. That room actually had a bunk bed in it, a full size bed on the bottom with a twin on top. Comes in handy when my friends and I would watch a game and drink a bit too much. The room wasn't quite as large as Connie's, but it was still pretty large, considering. It also didn't have it's own bath, but the hall bath was next door so it wasn't that much of an imposition. My own room had a large bath, complete with a sauna tub, separate shower, and separate toilet. What? I like my comfort. That's all.

Technically I had one more bedroom, but I used it as more of a large closet. Shelves along all the walls, tubs of gear stored along the bottom, that kind of stuff. My library was in there too. I had a fold up bed standing in one corner, but. . .it really wasn't up for occupancy except in an emergency.

I had put a lot of work into this place over the years I'd owned it. I'd gotten lucky with the house and I've never pretended otherwise. It was originally part of a small farm with right at two hundred acres. When I bought the place, I'd turned right around and sold the farm land apart from the two acres I'd kept for myself and used that to pay off the loan against the place. I didn't have money left over or anything but I was thrilled to have my place at what was essentially no charge. What would have gone toward paying for the mortgage was instead put into the house and property.

Anyway, Not So Bubbly Red Rita went into that third room. She was obviously not impressed with the accommodations, but. . .tough. She'd used all my patience already with her whiny ass attitude so I wasn't really feeling sympathetic. I was already planning to use her as bait the first time the zombies had us backed into a corner.

I know, I know. I'm going to hell for that one. Still, if it was choose between her and the doc, well. . .I'd shoot *myself* if I thought I had to spend the rest of my life with just Rita for company. Seriously, it was that bad.

I hoped that she might be one of those who would steady up if the shit hit the fan but there was no way to know until and unless the fan was actually hit. Until it did, I'd have to hope for the best and be prepared for the worst. Hence the plan in place to use her as zombie bait.

Stop judging me! You haven't had to sit in the same room with her while she lamented her damn dishes and wash stand and dolls and, and, and! I'm telling you, if you had to endure it, you'd have the same attitude I had. You cannot imagine. . . .

All right, enough about that. If you don't have the point by now, then I'm wasting my time. Moving on.

Anyway, that night Connie and I went over our loosely made plans checking our work, then checking behind each other. As far as we could tell we were okay, at least for now. I planned to clean and paint the cistern the next day and get it filled by the day after that. We'd have some water, if and when the utilities failed. Once I was finished, all I would have to do was check the gutter system to make sure we could switch it over once the water stopped.

I had plenty of filters for my filtration unit and the solar pump was in good shape. I didn't have a spare, but I did have enough PV equipment to replace it if I had to. Best I could do on short notice. I really wished we had a well, but two attempts to find water on the place had failed. I'm sure the farmer had suffered more than once for a lack of a well, but you can't put a well where there's no ground water.

If all else failed there was a creek behind my house right at the edge of my property. It usually had water. We could make the trek there to get water and then boil it to make it safe for drinking. Not the best option considering what we were preparing for, but like I said, last resort.

Otherwise we seemed to be on top of things. Connie had ordered some drugs she thought she'd need and had taken two suitcases full of bandages, supplies and equipment out of her office that afternoon. She'd do the same thing again that next day. She was trying to think ahead to what ever she might need and have that ready. Like I said, she was just as smart as she was good looking. And she was very good looking.

While we did this Rita was constantly droning in the background, whining about her room, her abandoned possessions, the necessity of being hunkered down in this 'miserable old farmhouse' and on and on and friggin' on. Once when I was probably about to explode, Connie reached under the table and squeezed my hand gently, and I relaxed. I looked at her, surprised, but she never looked up, just smiled slightly when she noticed me looking from the corner of her eye.

Busted again. Not that I cared. I couldn't be the only man who'd ever taken any possible opportunity to stare at her, know what I'm saying? The pressure of her knee against mine wasn't at all unpleasant, either.

I'll never know what made me think of gardening right then. Never will. There are a few ideas in my mind, but I'm not going to share them since they'll make me seem like all I had on my mind was Connie and. . .well, you think about it. It'll come to you.

Regardless, I suddenly realized that I hadn't picked up the least bit of seed, fertilizer, nothing. Be damn hard to plant a garden without them. I also realized I needed some heirloom seeds. I'd never bothered with them before because I really didn't have the extra time to set the seed aside and ready it for the next year's planting. That would have to change if this happened the way we were afraid it would.

Connie and I made a list of the seeds we'd most like to have, and I resolved to head into town again come morning and pick up all of them I could find, along with fertilizer. Realizing we had overlooked something so important made us start over on the lists, looking harder this time. We spent another hour trying to visualize anything that we might need, might have to make or repair, anything that could go wrong. We hadn't missed much, but what we had missed would matter.

Finally we were convinced we'd covered everything. I knew we hadn't and she probably did too, but there comes a point when you have to just stop for a while. It had been a long day already and we'd spent hours working over our plans. With red eyes we decided to stop for the night. Everyone was hungry, and Rita had been complaining about that for nearly an hour. Why she didn't just fix something I don't know. She was supposed to be a good cook.

I put on some beans and mixed up a pan of cornbread. Connie put some bacon on the griddle and then watched over the bread and beans while I started frying some diced potatoes. Simple food, but very good and filling. Surprisingly, I heard not one word of admonishment from the medical professional about healthy eating. Either she was hungry or she liked southern cooking as much as I did.

Rita looked askance at the meal when it was on the table. I'd made some tea, and when she found out I used saccharin to sweeten it she refused to drink it. 'Okay by me', I'd assured her. More for me.

She didn't like the water, it tasted funny. That wasn't possible I told her, since all my drinking water was run through a filter. One of the best available in fact. I used it to cook with, too. What tasted funny was that she was used to drinking treated water that still tasted like chemicals. I explained all that, and of course that just made her more angry still. Finally I just ignored her and ate.

Dreaming all the while about how nice it would be to shoot her in the head. I wasn't going to of course, but I really, *really* wanted to. Connie knew it, I guess, since she kept rubbing her knee against mine under the table. That was distracting me.

It also made me wonder if that's *all* she wanted to do, or if maybe, just *maybe*, she liked me back a little. I mean, you know, as more than just a friend or fellow survivor. *Oh*, how I wanted to believe that.

When we'd finished eating Connie smiled sweetly and asked if I minded doing the dishes. I told her I didn't, I was used to doing them anyway. She nodded and rose, asking Rita to come with her. The two went outside while I worked to clear my kitchen.

I suppose it's an oxymoron for most women, but despite the fact that I'm a man I kept a clean house. And my kitchen was kept even cleaner. I had a thing about germs, and keeping a clean house, especially the kitchen and bathrooms, was the best way I'd found to make sure that I didn't pick up anything that I couldn't wash off with Dial.

As I washed I was sure I heard raised female voices once or twice, but I chose to ignore it. Whatever was going on was between them was their business. Once I was finished I headed to the small fourth bedroom and put away the new re-loading supplies I'd gotten. I kept an old stand-up refrigerator for that, using air-dry to keep the moisture out. Pretty good powder safe if you can find one with a lock on it. I stored all the components in there then locked it back. Next I unpacked the new ammunition I'd bought, storing it in the small closet which I'd converted to what was essentially a walk-in gun safe and ammo storage area.

I was actually pretty happy with that, just to brag a little. The wooden door was still there, but it was only a cover. Inside the door was quarter-inch steel plate hung on very sturdy hinges. Three locks secured that steel door, which opened out rather than in. It had taken some tricky work to recess that door so that the wooden door could stay as camouflage.

Inside the closet, the same quarter-inch plate lined the walls, ceiling, and floor, welded together and then braced in the corners. A hand made gun rack dominated the long wall, with solid shelves over that to hold accessories and equipment. Oxygen absorbing elements were all over, keeping the closet moisture free as well.

It wasn't as fancy as some but it worked. It was secure, controlled, and perfect for me. Once I'd finished putting the ammo away, I checked the magazines I kept loaded. The dates were still okay (you don't leave a magazine loaded forever since it will weaken the spring. I dated mags when I loaded them with one of those small price stickers. After six weeks, I emptied them and loaded others) so I left them alone except for three, which I took to go with a Ruger Mini-14 I took from the rack. I picked up a bag for the rifle as well and then shut the door, locking it once more.

Now, I know what you're thinking. Why a Mini-14? Why not an AR platform. Well, there are a few reasons, actually, but the main one was simple. While a Mini-14 might not be quite as accurate as an AR, or as sexy, it would shoot any ammo that you could get into it, whereas an AR is balky about what ammo it would feed. I don't like balky. I like dependable. And my Ruger, or Rugers since there's more than one, were dependable.

Anyway, I figured it couldn't hurt to start putting a rifle in the vehicle when I was going into town. Hopefully if something happened here it was still a good ways off, but I didn't know that. Better to have and not need, right? I stored the bag with the rifle and mags in the hall closet, available for me to grab on my way out.

As I closed the door Connie and Rita came walking back in. Rita had been crying it looked like and I was almost sure that one side of her face was redder than the other. She mumbled something that might have been 'excuse me' as she moved past, heading straight to the room she was using and closing the door. I looked at Connie, who was smiling. It was a little cold I thought, that smile.

"I think Rita will be fine in the morning," she said very business like. Like a doctor who had treated a patient. "She's not coping as well as I'd thought, apparently. She's seeing now that this isn't some kind of game. She needs a night to sleep on it, that's all." With that Connie went to her own room, likewise closing the door behind her.

How 'bout that, huh? No good night. No 'thanks for supper, Drake'. No nothing.

Women, man. Almost as hard to figure as zombies sometimes.

CHAPTER FIVE

I was up the next morning by four-thirty. I'm usually an early riser, and once I'm awake that's it. I'm awake and I won't be able to go back to sleep. I envy those who can, since I almost always want to and I just can't.

Up, through the shower and with coffee perking, I fired up my computer and started surfing for news. While the story still hadn't broken containment, I had been right about the number of villages that were 'temporarily' cut off in Europe. People were starting to demand answers that the EU and it's member governments didn't want to give. Questions like why the roads were still blocked when in some cases the rock slide had happened over a week prior. Like why are the communications still down? In the modern era of digital communications there was no real reason, technically anyway, why the communication issues hadn't been cleared up. These were just the most pressing of the two questions now being asked not only by the people but the press as well.

Government officials were stammering and stuttering but not really answering the questions. That would work only so long before people started asking in a more determined way. Already three people had been 'detained' for trying to hike into one isolated town to check on family members. Like as not they would have disappeared but for the fact that one of them had the presence of mind to record the conversation live while uploading it to a cloud server. It was still streaming over YouTube and several other channels when the plug had been pulled. The damage was done, however, and the three had been taken into custody and detained in a very high profile way. If something happened to the two women and one man, questions would be asked. Lawyers were already working to have them released, and experts were saying there was no way to hold them much longer without creating a crisis.

Not my problem I admitted, but it did mean that control was slipping away from the authorities. I wished I could be listening in on conversations inside my own government, just to know what was being said and decided. I didn't figure they had any real answers either but knowing what they planned to do might have made it easier on me.

Other than the three detainees and some sporadic protests over the situation in general there were no new videos out of Europe. On the one hand I wanted to see more of what was happening but on the other hand the first video had been scary enough. I couldn't decide if the absence of more was a blessing or a curse.

On a whim I decided to check the message boards that I frequented on occasion. Much as I had expected, talk and rumor were rampant among the world's dedicated survival community. There were slips of news reports, most of which I'd already seen, along with a few eyewitness accounts and 'friend of a friend' type warnings and alerts, but no hard evidence. No one who had a copy of the Spain video was willing to put it up on the web for fear it would lead to a 'scrubbing' such as the one in Europe. Couldn't blame 'em for that. Most were willing to e-mail people they knew a copy so it was still getting around, just not in the open.

There were constant topics of advice. What to stock, what to buy now, what to try and scavenge later, the kind of people you wanted to surround yourself with. Most of it was sound advice. The ones that made me laugh though were the threads on *'how to combat the undead menace'* or *'dealing with zombies in a SHTF scenario'* and a dozen more just like them.

Seriously? Who's a friggin' expert on zombie combat? No one, that's who. What a load of horse shit! *'When approaching someone you know who may be infected, call them by name to see if they respond'*. Really? Hell, I was gonna do that anyway. *'If attacked, remember that the zombie can only be killed by a massive head wound that will render the re-animated brain activity to non-responsive'*. Who the hell talks like that? And where did they get that little gem of knowledge?

From movies, that's where. They took the shit from a movie and then dressed it up with some four dollar words, cleaned up the sentence structure, then threw it on the 'net. Here we were, possibly facing the Zombie Apocalypse End-of-the-world as we know it, and we're getting advice from George Romero fans? Shaking my head in sadness I left the forums behind, moving on to US news that might hint that the infections had spread to us.

After forty-five minutes of surfing I was pretty certain that nothing in the morning headlines indicated that the sickness had reached our shores yet. Of course that could change five minutes after I logged off, but I couldn't just sit here and monitor the web. I had work to do and errands to run, like it or not. I turned the computer off and got up. So many idiots and so few subjects for them to discuss this morning.

I spent the next half-hour making breakfast of pancakes, scrambled eggs, and sausage. As I cooked the eggs I realized that chickens should be on that list. Which meant I had to build a hen house, and lay in a supply of feed. And corn to stretch the feed.

It never ends, I thought to myself as I scratched a note on the bottom of the new list Connie and I had agreed on last night. I needed to get this done today if at all possible. I wondered how much help Bubbly Red Rita would be today, and decided probably not much. It also hit me that I'd have to leave her alone in my house if she didn't go anywhere and that was something I didn't want to do. I decided right there that I wasn't going to. She would have to go with me or go help Connie at the clinic. She wasn't staying here. She could always go to her own place for the day, I figured. Whatever she decided, she wasn't staying here without me around. That was just not gonna happen.

As I finished setting the table, Connie came around the corner and my breath caught for a second. Clearly she'd forgotten where she was since she was still in her sleep wear. Why was that a problem? Well, technically it wasn't. It was just that a string shoulder tank top and very brief, uh, briefs, really stood out on her. And other things stood out on her, too. I had to spin back around to the stove to keep her from seeing my reaction. She probably wouldn't have noticed since she was still half-asleep. She sat down, yawning, and looked at the table.

"Wow, Drake, you sure know how to spoil a girl," she smiled sleepily.

"Hey, nothing too good for my favorite roomie ever," I managed not to stutter a single time. Proud of me? Thank you.

"I'm not really a morning person, as you can probably tell," she admitted, taking the offered cup of coffee gratefully. "Thank you."

"You're quite welcome," I assured her, valiantly trying not to stare at all that cleavage, along with the very thin fabric covering, almost, her erect nipples. Oh man, was it hot in that kitchen? I must have left the stove on.

She noticed me trying not to notice and laughed a little.

"Are you uncomfortable?" she teased.

"Not really," I admitted. "Just trying to retain my gentleman upbringing, that's all," I looked her right in the face when I spoke, too. Damn, I am just *that good*, that's all.

"It's all right," she laughed again. "Like you said, we're roommates. You'll see me like this sooner or later."

"I'm in no way complaining my Queen," I bowed humbly, and was rewarded with a peel of laughter as she lightly slapped my shoulder.

"Stop that, I'm too grumpy this early to laugh!"

"As you wish, your mightiness," I bowed again, then thought about how much that sounded like 'nightdress', which of course she wasn't wearing. I'm telling you, I was beginning to think I wasn't going to make it to the Zompocalypse with all this. . .damn. Just *damn*.

And of course Rita came in just then ruining the whole damn thing. If I didn't already hate her, that would have done it right there. She was dressed frumpy and her hair was sticking out all over, so I assumed she's actually just awakened. She sat down at the table and started fixing a plate without so much as a 'thank you' or 'may I?' Rude bitch.

She was definitely going to be zombie bait if the need arose. Absolutely.

*****

Once breakfast was finished, me doing the dishes while Connie got ready for work and Rita apparently went back to bed, I took up my list and got ready to go. I walked down the hall to Rita's room and knocked on the door.

"What is it?" I heard the muffled answer.

"We're about to leave, Rita," I said evenly. "Are you about ready to go?" There was the sound of someone getting out of bed and stalking to the door, which opened abruptly.

"Go where?" she demanded crossly.

"Well, you can go with me to gather this new list of seed and garden needs and a few other odd and ends, or you can probably tag along with Connie to the clinic if you'd rather."

"I'll just stay here," she rolled her eyes, and started to shut the door. I caught it, and her eyes widened perceptibly.

"That's not an option," I told her flatly. "You're not staying here while I'm away. This is my home and I don't want anyone inside it while I'm gone. I'll be activating the alarm anyway and it would go off every time you moved."

"Well, just leave it off!" she snapped. "I'm not going anywhere!"

"You're either going with me, with Connie, or going home, Rita," I told her evenly. "And those are your options. You aren't staying here alone in my house. Not. Going. To happen." She looked at me goggle eyed for a minute, then her eyes narrowed in anger.

"I didn't want to come here in the first place!" she all but yelled.

"Then you shouldn't have," I shrugged. "Get your things together and I'll help you get moved back to your apartment. Shouldn't take us long. Maybe two hours or so."

"I'm not moving back this morning!"

"Then you can load your things in your car and sit in a parking lot," I told her, my own temper coming to a boil. "So far all you've done is whine and complain about everything without lifting a hand to do anything. You haven't offered to cook a meal, wash a dish, take out the trash, pick up items we need to be prepared, nothing. You've contributed nothing to this effort but problems and complaints and I'm sick and tired of it, understand? Now, you know your options. Pick one and let's be about it." I walked away at that point, too mad to keep talking to her.

Connie had stepped out of her room as my voice had raised and shot me a raised eyebrow look. I shrugged.

"She's not staying here while I'm away. I don't trust her as far as I can bowl her. She can go with me, with you, or home, and right now I'd prefer home so much that I'll help her move. I'm not trying to be difficult, but she's not contributing anything to the effort to start with. Leaving her here with my house is a non-starter. That's just the way it is. I'm sorry," I added, since I figured it might damage my relationship with the good doctor. If it did, it did. Connie just shook her head.

"Let me get dressed and I'll talk to her," she offered. "She'll do one of them, I promise. And I'm the one who's sorry, since I brought this on you. I really thought I knew her better," she apologized.

"It's all right," I sighed. "If she'll pull her weight and lose the attitude, I don't mind her staying. But the way she is right now, I'd rather she go even if it means you being mad at me and going too. I really don't want that, though," I said truthfully. She smiled softly.

"I'm staying right here," she informed me solidly. "Rita can do as she pleases, but I'm not going anywhere. If she moves back to the apartment, I might talk to you about making this permanent if I can keep this wonderful bedroom."

"Any room you want," was all I could manage before my tongue refused to work anymore. Permanent? Well, that was just, just. . .*awesome!*

I admit I might have whistled a little as I went to hitch up the trailer to my van for the trip into town. Just a little, mind you.

I wasn't out the door before the arguing started.

*****

Maybe twenty minutes later, Not-so-Bubbly Red Rita came stomping out of the house with an armload of her things, stalking to her car where she literally threw them inside. I watched her go back for more as Connie came out with another arm load.

"I take it she's going back?" I asked, and Connie nodded.

"Yes and I'm grateful for it," she huffed. "Stupid bitch. Thinks that she should be able to just lay around and have us take care of her. Damn, how did I get her so wrong?"

"Sometimes it happens," I shrugged philosophically. "What are you going to do?"

"I've already called the office," she replied. "I don't have an appointment until ten. If you don't mind, we'll just go to my apartment and get the rest of my things loaded on the trailer. I'm not staying with her and I'm not about to leave my things there for her to chuck out into the parking lot. I've already called the manager and told him I'll keep paying the balance of the lease until it's open, but I won't be in residence." She looked up at me, eyes dark with concern.

"Are you sure this is okay, Drake?" she asked seriously. "I mean, me staying here? It's a big deal, and once I'm committed then I have to stay here until that lease is paid. It's too high for me to afford another place that's not in the ghetto."

"I'm *positive* it's okay," I nodded, fighting off a grin. "So long as you let me take you to dinner, and maybe a movie. Just in case the world as we know it does come crashing down at some point, I'd really like to be able to say I dated you at least once," I admitted and didn't even blush when I said it. She laughed lightly.

"You are completely single minded, you know that?" she smiled.

"Where you are concerned, I guess I am," I admitted.

"I'd like that," she said softly, her smile softening as well. "I really would. Maybe tomorrow night?"

"It's a date," I nodded firmly. "Meanwhile, let's get Miss Congeniality out of our hair for good."

*****

It took an hour to get Rita back home, and another hour-and-a-half to get Connie packed to go. The hardest part was her furniture, a bedroom suite and recliner along with an entertainment center, large flat-screen and surround sound stereo movie player combination. It all fit in the trailer with a little room to spare though. During the packing Rita continued to snipe at both of us but we ignored her, satisfied to be rid of her stupid ass.

At one point she threatened to tell everyone in town what we'd shared with her about the possible zombie problem. Both of us stopped at that, looking at her. She obviously hadn't expected that reaction and began to back-track. I held up a hand to stop her and moved to face her.

"If you were to do something like that," I said evenly, "how do you think it will look when we explain the truth about why Connie moved out and left you here?" Rita frowned, but I went on. "You know, how you started seeing all kinds of crazy conspiracy things in the news, on the internet, and started losing your grip on reality. We tried an intervention, but it failed. Since you hadn't done anything illegal or threatened yourself or anyone else we couldn't really report you, but Connie had to think about her career so she did the only thing she could and moved. Since she can't afford to pay for this place and another one, she moved in with a friend, me, until the lease here was up and she could find a place of her own somewhere else."

"Meanwhile, we were trying to see if we could get you some help involuntarily, since you wouldn't go on your own. I'd imagine once you start spreading that crap of yours, the involuntary part will come along pretty quickly, don't you?" I finished and stood back, waiting. And maybe smirking a little bit.

"I'm willing to bet your company wouldn't want it known that one of their reps was losing her grip on reality, either," Connie added calmly, catching on nicely. Rita's face flushed.

"You can't threaten me!" she retorted.

"Why not?" I asked. "You threatened us just now. How's it feel, by the way?"

"But I would be telling the truth!" she shot back, and seemed to take strength from that.

"As far as you're able to tell truth from fiction these days," I said with a sad tone of voice. Fake, of course. "We're really concerned about you, but can't find a way to help you. It's a shame, really. You're not a bad person, just. . .confused. That's all." At that point I stopped play acting.

"You breathe a word against us Bubbly, and we'll bury you. You'll be lucky to stay out of the nut-house, let alone keep your cushy job. Got that?"

Red faced and trembling in anger Rita stormed away, walking outside. I followed to the door to make sure she didn't try and molest the van or trailer but she got into her car and screeched away.

"Let's get this done and away from here," Connie said sadly into the silence. "She's lost it."

Twenty hard minutes later Connie made a final walk though, making sure she had everything. That done, we left, her going to work and me back to the house to leave the trailer.

I left the van and trailer at home and took Big Baby to get the stuff we needed. We never did see Rita again after that. No idea what happened to her, to be honest. Maybe she made a relief center somewhere. If they were still working. The one person we'd tried to help, and that was the thanks we got. See what I mean? How can you help people when the world responds like that? I wish I could say she was an exception, but. . .she's not. If you present a problem to someone and it's out of their comfort zone, they'll like as not turn it around on you.

And that's probably why the world went to hell in a hand-bag, you know?

*****

I made it back home just in time, since the Fed-Ex guy rolled into the yard less than thirty minutes after I got back with the seed and other items. It wasn't the regular guy I noticed and soon learned why. Almost the entire truck was filled with just our two orders.

"You folks getting ready for the End Times?" the guy asked, laughing. I joined him.

"No, something worse," I told him. "Summer camp." He joined me in a good laugh as I helped him unload the goods into my garage. "Just leave it here," I told him. "Won't be here long."

"Well, I guess you're set then," he said when we finally finished, offering me the signing doo-hickey. I signed and handed it back.

"Yeah. Hopefully we won't have another round of mumps and measles this year," I added, shaking my head. "Dealing with kids you never know what you're gonna get. Thanks for getting this here so fast."

"Name of the game," the driver nodded, returning to his truck. "Have a good weekend!"

"You too!" I called back. "Drive safe!" He waved once more and then headed out. I watched him go, proud of my act. I guess it's a little deceptive of me, but I really didn't want people asking too many questions. I might not want to answer them.

I got a tarp and covered the boxes over completely. My small shop was now a thing of the past until and unless we moved all this stuff. I wanted to make sure we could get the van inside the garage in case of emergency. Say we got surrounded by zombies, then we could at least get to the van safely, and maybe escape. Last resort, of course, but no sense in taking chances.

With all the orders in, all the supplies on hand, fence checked and strengthened, fuel tanks filled and so on, it was time to tackle the cistern. I hated the thought of it but it had to be done. As a result I spent the rest of the day pumping the stagnant water out, blowing it dry (leaf blowers are great), and painting the floor and walls with the same paint used on swimming pools. It was treated with some kind of 'safe' chemical, probably chlorine, that was supposed to keep algae from growing on the surfaces. It had cost a small fortune so I hoped it worked.

While the paint was drying I checked my gutter system. They were surprisingly clean and clear of obstruction. I wouldn't use the gutters unless and until we lost the city water supply, but if that happened then we'd be glad to have the water it provided. Meanwhile I had a rain collection system of barrels and tanks already and used that water for the yard, the garden, and washing my vehicles.

By the time that was finished the day was beginning to wane and I was filthy. It had been a long day. I checked the cistern and found the paint was nearly dry. I closed it off but left the vent open to allow the paint fumes to escape. It was screened so there wasn't much risk of anything getting inside. I had planted citronella plants around the cistern to keep down mosquitoes and so far they had worked well. Smart huh? Okay, I read about it online. But still, I did the work. Besides, there's nothing wrong with learning from other people so long as they aren't idiots.

Or liberals.

Anyway, I was tired and in need of a shower so I headed inside. I set some steaks out of the freezer though I didn't know for sure what Connie might want to do for supper. I was sort of floating along right now. She was living in my house and we had an honest to goodness date tomorrow night, but. . .calmly, Drake. Calmly.

I really didn't want to mess things up. There was no such thing as too slow where she was concerned. Not at this point. She knew I wanted her, but hell every straight man she'd ever met wanted her. She also knew by now that I wanted more than that, and maybe that was the difference. I sure hoped so. She literally took my breath away.

I got cleaned up and changed, then headed out into the living room. Connie was pulling into the yard as I stepped outside, and smiled when she saw me. That was enough to keep me going another day right there. She looked tired but otherwise okay.

"How was your day?" she asked and even gave me a little peck on the cheek. Heaven!

"Went very well and just got better," I smiled. "Food's here, in the garage. Cistern is ready, gutters are too, and the seed, fertilizer and other odds and ends are unloaded and put away."

"Wow, you really got things done didn't you?" she smiled again. "Nothing like a hard working man," she sighed a little, and I felt my feet levitate off the floor. She had to know the effect she was having on me. Not that I cared.

"Well, better to get it done and over with," I said honestly. "I like my loafing time as much as the next man, but I loaf better when the work's all done."

"Smart man," she nodded. "Let me get cleaned up and changed. How about we go out, tonight? I don't know about you, but I could use a good steak and maybe a trip to the mall to walk around and look at the world." She looked at me seriously. "Might not get many more chances to do something like that if this thing gets out of hand."

I admitted that was true, and agreed it was a good idea. I put the steaks I had laid out back in the freezer, figuring they would be there another time. Forty-five minutes later Connie walked out of her room looking like a model on the runway. My mouth tried to water and go dry at the same time, leaving me choking and coughing.

"Are you okay?" she asked, smirking a little.

"Fine," I croaked back. "Just fine."

*****

We hit the town quietly but with eagerness. First order of the night was Connie's good steak. We dined quietly, no talk of any zombies, Rita, the possible end-of-the-world, nothing like that. Connie told me a little bit more about herself, about her time with Doctors Without Borders. She really was nothing short of amazing.

When it was my turn I had nothing so interesting to share. I had worked my way through college by doing what was known as contractor work. I guess I never mentioned what I did for a living, did I? My bad. I'm in computers. Sort of a fireman for computer systems. During summer breaks and slow times, I picked up unofficial money by working for companies that were contracted to Uncle Sam. Sometimes I cleaned up systems that had been attacked by foreign countries, sometimes I returned the favor. The pay for things like that was surprisingly good and almost always 'off the record', which was govspeak for 'cash'.

Now I worked for a private firm that structured system security for some of the largest corporations in the U. S. and Canada. Sometimes I had to travel a lot, but it was always on the company's dime and I had seen some really nice places that I'd otherwise probably never gotten to see. I'd made a good living over the last decade. I'd miss it if the world went to hell. All that work to get somewhere.

Anyway, we had a good time getting to know one another better. After dinner we went on to the mall. Usually the mall was one of those places I wouldn't be seen dead, but. . .Connie wanted to go, and that meant that I wanted to go, too. Know what I mean? I know, I know, and you're right. What can I say though?

The mall wasn't overly crowded like it usually seemed to be. I mean there was a good crowd there, don't get me wrong, it just didn't seem like the wall-to-wall people that I usually saw when I had to come here.

We made a round on the first floor before taking the escalator upstairs. Connie had her arm through mine, which added at least three inches to my height and earned me a mall full of admiring looks from the men who got a good look at her. Ah, me. I was getting my man card filled with all this public attention.

We were about half-way down the second floor when my phone buzzed gently in my pocket. I almost ignored it, but decided to check since it might be important. My house alarm sent an alert to my phone when it activated after all.

It wasn't my alarm.

I had set several e-mail alerts for key words and phrases to monitor from news sources. I had gotten a hit. I pulled Connie over to the side, finding a place in the open doorway of a Dillards that kept the crush of people off of us, and opened the alert.

One of the 'isolated' villages in Europe, this one in Germany, had been filmed by an enterprising news crew that had apparently gotten wind that something was wrong in Denmark. Well, Germany. I already used that pun didn't I? Sorry.

Anyway, they had hiked in after getting close on snowmobiles, and set up on a ridge overlooking the town. I can't recall the name of the place, but it looked like a permanent Oktoberfest kind of place, you know?

Well, it *had,* anyway. Connie and I huddled around the small screen of my phone and watched the video. Apparently this had been a real news team, because the video was clean and clear and the narration was pretty good. Not that we needed it after they finally got the camera on the town center.

It was like that video from Spain all over again, writ larger. This German town was pretty good sized, maybe ten, fifteen thousand people, and it looked like most of them were sick. Or whatever this was. I really didn't know, to be honest. Whatever they were, the town was wrecked. Several fires were burning across the town's skyline. And despite the official statement that utilities had been interrupted by the rock slide/avalanche/freak ice storm/whatever else the powers that be had come up with, the lights were definitely still on in this town.

As the video played we could see flashes below, and the camera operator zoomed in on those. After some movement to search the area, the camera steadied up on three uniformed figures dressed in military gear and carrying what looked like GS-3 rifles, at one time the preferred rifle of the West German forces and later the reunified German Wehrmacht. They were a little long on tooth for modern times but were likely still in use in their reserves, and civilian models were probably available.

Whoever they were, and wherever they had gotten the rifles, the three people were on a shooting spree in the town center. Two shooting and one loading all the time made me think they weren't just your average Germans, either. That was good training, and it was holding despite the fact that the trio was surrounded by villagers who were probably trying to eat them. Okay, that was an assumption, but hey, all I had to go one was movies and books, you know?

As we watched, one of the shooters must have run dry. He fixed a bayonet and took up a defensive stance, using a fence at his back for security. He tried to guard the backs of the two still shooting, but forgot to watch his own. Connie and I watched without comment as he was pulled over the fence and into the waiting arms of at least three 'people'. I really, even then, didn't want to use the z-word.

That left two. They lasted maybe another minute until both ran dry at the same time. In seconds they were overrun. As I watched their attackers pile on, I didn't even want to imagine what was happening at the bottom of that pile.

The news crew made a few comments as they panned the village a few more time, but found nothing else of interest. Having done what they came to do, they wisely beat feet, humping back the way they had come, camera still recording along with their sound system. They didn't shut them down even once they mounted their snow mobiles and took off, running for safety. As the video ended, I shut off the program and looked at Connie. She was white-faced and I was sure her hand was shaking.

"That 'll do it, probably," I told her softly. "Once this starts making the rounds, someone is gonna have to own this or the riots and demonstrations will be hard to deal with." She nodded.

"What should we do?" she asked, looking around us as if we could expect zombie hordes at any moment. I thought about it a minute, but the truth was there was nothing else we could do. We'd made all the preparations we could. Only time would tell if they were enough.

"We should have a good time," I told her calmly. "By tomorrow, this is going to be everywhere. And there's no telling what will happen then. We might as well enjoy what will probably be the last normal night in this town for quite a while." She looked surprised at first, but as my words sank in she smiled.

"We might as well at that," she said after a minute. "I'm glad you're with me, Drake," she said softly. "I really am. Despite everything, I'm actually having a good time."

"I'll take that as a compliment since I desperately want one from you," I winked and she laughed, which was what I was hoping for. Then, arm-in-arm, we continued our night at the mall.

I was sure that tomorrow would be full of panic and speculation. We were already as prepared as we could be. All we could do now was wait and I preferred waiting in the mall in the company of the most beautiful woman I'd ever known.

Even with the end-of-the-world maybe approaching, I was having a pretty good night. And who knew? It might get better still.

CHAPTER SIX

I had been right.

Connie and I finished up our impromptu date night with desert at the food court and decided to catch a late movie at the theater across the parking lot. I purposely ignored the phone after that, refusing to let my curiosity ruin my evening. I endured a chic flick with Connie, something she wanted to see that I can't for the life of me remember the name of and I don't care really. I would have sat through a speech by Hillary Clinton if Connie Kane had asked me to. There was no danger of that of course since my wonderfully gorgeous doctor roommate was thoroughly conservative.

Anyway, we got home late, almost midnight. Both of us were exhausted as it had been a very long day. Connie actually kissed me on the cheek as she headed for her room.

"I had a really nice time, Drake," she said softly, and I will always believe that her eyes were shining a little despite how tired she was. "Thank you."

"It was absolutely my pleasure," I assured her. "Sleep well."

I hit the shower, cold this time (shut up), and then racked out. I think I was asleep when I hit the pillow, the work of the day catching up to me at last.

As usual I was up right before dawn. Still tired but like I said before, once I'm up, that's it. I ran through the shower one more time just to help me get fully awake and then headed for the living room, stopping in the kitchen long enough to put on some coffee.

I fired up my computer, wondering what I would see after last night's video. I fully expected to see dramatic headlines sporting titles like 'Government officials deny any knowledge of zombie horde sweeping through Europe'.

Well, it wasn't that bad, but I wasn't disappointed.

Believe it or not there was still an attempt at denial even in the face of the video from the night before. Stuffed suits making the rounds were intercepted by reporters demanding to know what was going on only to be told that the 'incident' was under investigation and comment would be 'inappropriate' until all the facts were 'in'. Usually that would have bought them a day, give or take twelve hours. Not today.

Reporters increased their demands to the point that officials stopped talking to them altogether, depending on security services to screen them from the press. Incensed, reporters then turned to looking for people who might have first hand knowledge of just what the hell was going on in all these isolated towns. Some of the people they interviewed were complete frauds of course and it was easy to tell who they were. Others were much more convincing. One in particular caught my eye. Well one aside from the interview with the crew that had provided the video we had seen last night.

A Spanish news wire broke the story first. A man had come forward with a video. I don't think I ever did learn his name, but the video was what mattered. It was the same video that had first caught my attention.

I listened to his interview, reading the subtitles as they scrolled across the screen. He had been working in a small butcher shop when a woman had stumbled into the front, bleeding from a wound on her shoulder. The owner of the shop had hurried forward to assist the woman, calling for his wife to summon the authorities. Even as the wife was dialing emergency services the owner screamed in pain.

The man had run from the kitchen at the commotion and was standing in the doorway when the woman had sank her teeth into the owner's neck. As he watched, she shook her head violently, ripping and tearing flesh from her victim. The man had hesitated only a second before grabbing the screaming wife and pulling her toward the back. As he made his way toward the back door the woman had ripped away from his grasp and ran back toward the shop front.

The man paused for a second, lips trembling, and I felt sorry for him. He was obviously smarting over his failure to keep her from going back to her husband, but I just didn't see that it was his fault. I mean, it was her *husband* man. Love makes you do crazy shit, that's just a fact.

Like running into the maw of a zombie horde.

He went on as the video began playing, describing what he had seen as he was running for his life, trying to record everything he could on his phone. That had confirmed my own suspicions about the video quality. He had made his way through town on foot, not owning a car. He'd never needed one, he said, always living right there in his home town just a few blocks from where he worked. When he wanted to go somewhere he took the bus.

The same bus that had saved his life that day. The driver had realized that something bad was happening though he hadn't a clue what it was. He had held the bus, door open, for as long as he dared, allowing as many people as possible to cram aboard including this man now speaking on the television. When 'they' started coming into view the driver had closed the door of the overloaded bus and stepped on the gas, speeding toward the next city and help.

They had met a number of police cars along the way and the man from the butcher shop had asked to be let off the bus long before the next town. The driver hadn't questioned him, probably because the bus was so crowded. The man had headed across country to his cousin's, where he had spent the night telling and re-telling his story. He hadn't known for almost a full day that his sudden urge to visit family might well have saved him, since that bus had not been seen or heard from again.

I admit that I stopped listening after that, leaning back in my chair. The bus hadn't been heard from again? How the hell did that happen? As soon as the question formed in my mind I knew the answer. Someone, somewhere, had decided that it was in their best interest that the people who had escaped from that hellish scene not be allowed to speak to anyone about it. This guy had gotten lucky on a grand scale, twice in the same day.

He should buy a lottery ticket.

I went back to the interview just as it was wrapping up, with the man stating that one reason he had agreed to come forward and tell his story was that he feared something had been 'done' with the bus and passengers and that he was afraid that if it was discovered he had been aboard he might disappear too, along with his extended family who had taken him in. He hoped that being in the public eye would prevent that, or at least make it less likely to happen.

Smart man, I nodded. Clearly this guy was smarter than the average politician. Or reporter.

The newsman conducting the interview then launched into a string of questions that this poor man had no way of answering; What was to blame for the behavior evident in the video? Had any of the townspeople been seen or heard from since? Why had the bus left before ensuring that everyone was safe? Did he feel guilty about leaving so many behind as he fled to safety?

What? Seriously? This man was running for his life from an unknown threat and this jackass reporter was asking him shit like this? Hadn't he already said the bus driver waited as long as possible before leaving? That the bus was dangerously overloaded? Had the reporter missed the part about people being dragged down in the street and. . .*dined on*? What a jackass!

The man never turned a hair at the reporter's attitude, waiting until the tirade was over before calmly explaining that he had no way to lend assistance to anyone. Strict and severe gun control laws in Europe had meant that he had no way to defend himself, let alone assist others. He had no skill in unarmed combat, no military training, no background that would lend itself to helping him or allowing him to help others. So he had fled for his life.

Just like everyone else was doing.

The reporter seemed to be taken aback by this calm reply and decided to change his tactic by asking yet another series of questions that this man couldn't possibly answer; What was the cause of this event? How had people been affected in the first place? Was it contagious and if so how was it spread? Did he have any advice for others who might find themselves in his situation? That last one the man answered. He looked directly into the camera and spoke three words.

"Run. And pray."

I ignored the rest of the crap from the reporter, dropping the site and looking at several web pages of written news reports. As I had predicted, people were up in arms this morning with demonstration in every nation where one of the 'isolated' towns was located. Police and in some cases military were being used to contain the protests, but in at least two places, one in Germany and the other in France, the police and military appeared to be siding firmly with the protesters. That was going to get interesting and quick.

An alert caught my eye and I pulled it up. "White House to make statement on European disturbance at noon, EST."

Well. That I hadn't seen coming. Since there were no reported problems in the States I guess I had assumed that there wouldn't be anything from our own government just yet. Which automatically made me wonder why there *was* going to be something from our own government.

Which made me question whether or not something *had* happened in the States and we just hadn't heard about it yet. Shit. Dammit. I had screwed up trusting that this was strictly a European problem for the present.

I knew better. Got no excuse except that I was so busy with other stuff. You know, like getting ready for the zombie apocalypse and shit like that. And we *were* ready I reminded myself before I started preparing for ritual suicide to atone for my failure. While I *might* have missed something happening here in the USA by ignoring the news last night, I took comfort in knowing that there wasn't a single thing I could have done that I hadn't already accomplished.

We were as ready as we could possibly be under the circumstances. Satisfied with that, I headed for the kitchen to start breakfast. This might be a long day.

By the time Connie came strolling into the kitchen I had a good breakfast ready. She smiled brightly despite her sleepy look, taking her seat and fixing a plate. As we ate I filled her in (yes, I know what I said) on what I'd learned already from the news.

"Noon, huh?" she mused from behind a piece of toast. "Wonder why noon? Think they're going to have a solution by then?"

"I doubt it," I told her with a snort. "No, it's probably so they can get their story straight. There's also the possibility that we've already had some trouble here in the States and they want to make sure that's under control before they talk about it. Other than that? Lunch time for those working today. People who are out and about may miss it all together if they're DGIs." Don't Get Its. People who simply cannot conceive of a world where the 'gubermint' would lie. Or even mislead if they thought it was in their, I mean the *country's*, best interest. Yeah, that's sarcasm.

"Well, I can't think of a thing we can do differently, can you?" she asked. I shook my head. I really couldn't. We had probably missed something, but neither of us had been able to find it.

"Then let's head into town, grab a few last minute things like paper goods and what have you, then plan to be back here for the big new conference," Connie said.

"Works for me," I nodded. I began gathering up the dishes while she went to get ready. By the time I was done she was back, and oh, man was she a picture.

T-Shirt, jean shorts that showed off a wonderful set of legs, hair pulled into a pony-tail. I stared a little too long I guess and she laughed at me.

"What?"

"Seriously?" I asked. "You *have* to know the effect you have on me," I all but blurted out. She smiled brightly at that.

"I'm glad to hear that," she told me and kissed my cheek again. "And I don't think I'll get tired of hearing it." With that she was out the door, a large bag over her shoulder. I admired the view for a few steps before I followed.

Zombies or not, my life was improving by the day.

*****

Town was a madhouse. Part of that was just because it was Saturday you know, but. . .some of it wasn't.

We drove through town once before we stopped anywhere. We decided to avoid the box marts for several reason, one being the huge crowds. We decided to visit the smaller chain stores and the locally owned places. The variety might be less and the prices a bit more but it was a tradeoff we were willing to pay for.

Connie stocked up on um. . .well, girl stuff. You know. I added many many rolls of toilet paper to the van, along with paper towels and some thicker more sturdy shop towels. Paper plates and plastic utensils made the buggy as well. Lighters, fluid, and matches. Scented candles. Just odd and end, world may be ending kind of stuff, you know.

We got canned soda and a lot of chips and junk food that were sealed in foil. A few favorite cookies and what not packaged the same way. Comfort food mostly. Might get a little stale over time, but spread out over a long period of time it might help fight food fatigue. You can get seriously sick of the same stuff day in and day out. Well, unless it's a Jack's Cheeseburger. Double Big Jack. Mustard, pickles, onions, lettuce. Fries but none of that cheese salt crap they use. I *hate* that stuff. Still the burgers more than make up for it.

We kept an eye on the time as we went, wanting to make sure we made it back in time for the 'noos'. We didn't take all of anything from anywhere we went. I hate people who do that, you know? Also it attracts attention. I had noted a few people giving us the eye, but they were guys and Connie looked good enough to eat (oh, I am *so* going to hell for that) so I cautiously wrote it off to them ogling her and not our stuff. Besides it wasn't like we had pallets of food or anything. To most people we should have looked just like any other two people shopping on a Saturday. Which we kinda were.

By eleven we had done about all we could think of. I wheedled Connie into stopping at Jacks so I could continue my slow suicide of unhealthy eating. She chose a salad and tea, but you know what I got. To her credit, Connie didn't harp at me over the completely unhealthy choices I had made. Maybe because she thought it might not be long until I couldn't get any more. Whatever the reason, I foundered myself on two, that's *two*, of my favorite all time non-homemade burgers and probably a half-gallon of Dr. Pepper. Well, a quart anyway.

We made our way home and unloaded everything into the house with about ten minutes to spare. By the time the conference started we were finished and sitting side-by-side on the couch.

There was the usual hub-bub at the first, 'grave situation', 'national significance', and the like. Finally though

Dumbo stepped onto the podium. I didn't like the guy, still don't for that matter, but I was honestly a little concerned at how drawn he looked. He usually looked a little more. . .well, I don't know. He looked tired. *Worn* was the word that floated around in my head to be honest.

"My fellow Americans," he started with the same line every President since Kennedy had used. *"You have no doubt seen the news reports from Europe this morning, or perhaps last evening. You no doubt have concerns about what you have seen and heard, and rightfully so. I have this morning, along with my staff and senior members of the Administration and with senior members of both the House and Senate, been in contact with our opposite numbers in the regions and nations affected by this unprecedented phenomenon."*

"European leaders assure me that they are taking all precautions possible to contain the problem and prevent its spread. After hearing their actions and their plans, we have to agree that they are doing all that can be done under the circumstances."

"At this time there is very little known about the virus that is causing this problem. Specimens have been taken for examination and both the U.S. Army's Medical Research Institute and the Center for Disease Control are assisting with the investigation aspect of this problem. As of yet however there is nothing to report that is not already in the public domain." He paused, looking around.

"It was decided in a meeting this morning with my senior advisers that we would present everything we know to the American people during this brief. There's simply no reason, no advantage, in withholding information. The truth is we don't have any idea what is causing this outbreak of violence outside that it is some kind of sickness. One that spreads with alarming speed by every account available."

"Contact with bodily fluids seems to be the only way the virus spreads, at least for the moment, but medical professionals are warning that viruses can and do evolve as their environment changes so we cannot depend upon, cannot count upon this staying the case. The method of spread may change and we must be aware of that danger."

"In just a moment the Surgeon General will present the symptoms of the virus as they are known to be at present, along with precautions that may help prevent its spread. Let me stress that at this time there are no known cases in the United States or American territories. That is not something we can count on to continue. Hopefully it will, but it would be irresponsible not to allow for contingencies in the event that the virus finds its way to our shores."

"Because this cannot fail to cause at least a momentary panic, I have, after consulting with Congressional leaders, closed the stock exchanges for the next few days. Banks will be open, but monetary withdrawals will be limited for the next few days as well. Normal business will be conducted without interruption but bank runs will not be allowed to happen. Prices on all commodities including gasoline are frozen for the immediate future. We will not tolerate price gouging or profiteering during this time of crisis."

"*Let me repeat that no cases of this virus have been reported or even suspected in the U.S. or her territories. It may be that none will be. But we will exercise precaution until such time as this current crisis is behind us. Use good judgment, common sense, and follow the protocols that are about to be disseminated to you. They are for your safety and are the best protection we have against contamination at this time. And now, the Surgeon General.*"

I tuned out the rest. Connie was taking notes as the S.G. rattled off his list of precautions. She was far more qualified than I was to think about that. I was thinking about the speech. There were several things that I just. . .I couldn't put my finger on it exactly but it just seemed *off*, somehow. *Wrong.*

I mean, Europe has a Zombie infestation and we're being cautioned to use common sense and good judgment? This administration had never once been guilty of trusting the good judgment and common sense of its citizens, yet suddenly we're on our own? And that's when it hit me.

We were on our own. He had basically just told us that it was every man for himself from here on out. Sure it was camouflaged with the diplospeak and just enough of actual truth to make it plausible, but no martial law? No rationing? No travel restrictions? There was just no way this was right!

"This is bullshit," Connie said suddenly, drawing me away from my introspection.

"What?"

"This is total bullshit," she held up the pad she'd been making notes on, nodding to the screen. "This is the standard drill for shit like the flu, Drake. I tell this stuff to patients every day. It's some of the oldest precautions known to medicine."

"So? I mean a reminder isn't a bad idea under the circumstances, right?" She was shaking her head.

"No, you don't understand. This should be treated as a Level Four quarantine. There's a whole different set of rules for that kind of thing. A virus that spreads through fluid contact, no vaccine, no cure, no Patient Zero, *nothing*. The precautions for something like this are through the roof. At a minimum we should see travel bans and curfews until this is under control. It's the best, safest way to try and prevent the spread of the virus."

"Well, that answers that, I guess," I leaned back, head resting on the back of the couch. She turned to face me, hooking one gorgeously tanned leg over the. . .*not now, not now, not now*, I told my traitorous inner voice. Anyway, she looked at me questioningly.

"There was no travel restrictions. No rationing, no curfew, nothing. Absolutely nothing. No precautions announced outside the financial sector and that's something that everyone would have expected. He just left the nation wide open to a mass panic and didn't announce a single precaution to prevent it. If we could see . . . ." I got up abruptly and went to get my laptop.

"Wh. . .what are you doing?" Connie demanded but I was already on my way back. I sat back down and brought up a camera from the courthouse in town, courtesy of the local paper.

"Look," I told her, turning the screen where she could see.

It had started already, people running to grab what they could from where they could. We watched for a few minutes before turning to a news channel from the nearest city.

There were already riots in the streets, fires burning out of control and people screaming about government conspiracies and biological attacks.

"That last might make sense," Connie admitted, looking at the notes she'd taken.

"Really?" I asked, surprised to say the least.

"Yes," she nodded. "I doubt that it is in all honesty, but it's always possible. It might be an engineered virus that escaped a lab where it was being developed. That happens a lot more than people might think," she told me flatly.

"Why do you doubt it's an actual attack?" I wanted to know.

"No locus," she replied, and I'm sure the dumb look on my face was what prompted her to explain.

"Look. A biological attack has to be widespread to do any real damage. It's too easy to cordon off an area or just firebomb the hell out of it to kill the virus and stop the spread. To prevent that, you have more than one release area. In fact you have a dozen or more if you can, all in public areas to infect as many people as possible. It guarantees the virus will survive and that you get the maximum possible spread of infected people. Who in turn carry the virus somewhere else and spread it further. All of that establishes patterns which in turn can be traced to precise locations of initial infection."

"Wow," was all I could think of to say, both about the facts she'd given me and the fact that she had them to start with. Be still my heart.

"Anyway, there's nothing like that here," she went on. "That makes it more likely that it's either naturally occurring or it's an accidental release. Either way, it's too spread out now to contain," she sighed, tossing her steno pad onto the table. "They can try a nuke, I guess. Or maybe carpet the areas with napalm. But otherwise, it's *out there.*"

"What?" she had my undivided attention now. Well, okay, she always had my undivided attention but now I was listening to what she was saying instead of just. . .anyway.

"Those are the only two sure fire ways to kill a virus," she shrugged. "Burn them up. I suppose there are some other napalm like mixtures they can use, but essentially it's all about the fire now. The only way to be sure is to hit it with high temperature flames."

I honestly didn't know what to say at that point. A nuke? Thermite maybe instead of napalm? I didn't know. I didn't think I *wanted* to know, either.

"Well, I guess now all our actions the last few days are justified," I sighed. "We're ahead of the crowd at least."

"I'm glad you came to see me," Connie nodded. "And that you trusted me," she added, leaning back on the couch against my shoulder. "I'd be running scared about now at best."

"I doubt it," I snorted, placing an arm around her shoulder. "You're too smart for that. You might be in a rush, but there's no way you'd be in a panic." She smiled up at me and kissed my cheek.

"I appreciate that. What do we do now?" she asked.

"Hell if I know," I admitted, and it was true. We were as ready as we could possibly be at this point. All we could do now was wait and see what happened. "It's Saturday, so I guess we'll see how things develop. Maybe there won't be any problems here, but. . .I get the feeling there's already a problem here. In America, I mean," I added.

"Why?"

"That speech sounded more like an ass covering stance than anything else," I pointed out, and it had. "It's almost as if they know they can't contain the problem and this was a way to hold off as much of the inevitable panic as possible. See what I mean?" She nodded thoughtfully at that.

"What do we do, though?" she asked again. "I mean, do we go to work Monday? Do we just hole up here from now on and wait and see? We've made about all the preparations we can make that I know of."

"I think so too," I admitted. "The only thing I know is to make sure we're always thinking. Looking around us, considering what we may need and the like. For instance, I had the idea. . .wow, maybe it was just yesterday. Anyway, I had the idea that we should get some chickens. Just a few, for eggs and for meat too, if things go on like we're afraid they will. I did get some feed and laying mash when I was in town."

"Well, let's go see if we can find some chickens, then," Connie got to her feet and held out a hand. "We're not getting any younger."

"No, I suppose not," I agreed and got to my feet as well. "Let's take some precautions, though. Things will be crazy now."

*****

Crazy indeed. Man it was like watching a Chinese fire drill in conjunction with a

Keystone Cops convention and throwing in one of those Shriner groups that did the crazy driving stunts in parades.

Cars were everywhere, running and gunning all over town as people scrambled to get this and that and whatever they could think of. There was a line at least twenty cars long at the local bank drive-through since the lobby was closed on Saturday.

"What a mess," Connie was shaking her head. "I didn't think it would be this bad this quick." Truthfully I hadn't either. I guess more people had been watching than I had thought. Or else word had traveled fast, I didn't know.

We rolled into the Co-op to a fairly calm scene. I used their pumps to fill up Big Baby, just in case. Meanwhile Connie was taking notes from their 'For Sale or Trade' board. When I got inside I noted that the young guy behind the counter was paying close attention to her. I didn't blame him of course, but I couldn't help feel a little tingle of jealousy. I managed to tromp on it as he turned reluctantly to me.

"Help you?" he asked, though you could tell he wished I had dropped dead rather than enter the store while he had Connie all to himself.

"He's with me," Connie called over her shoulder and I grew at least six inches taller while the pimply faced little shit behind the counter deflated. *'Served the little prick right'*, I thought with malicious glee.

"Find anything?" I asked, careful not to smirk at Pimply as I walked by.

"Yeah, a few," Connie nodded, still writing. "Chickens, a few geese and ducks, even some small pigs."

"I know nothing whatever about butchering a pig," I admitted. "Not against the idea, just don't know how. Also we don't really have a place to keep one."

"Well, I don't really care about the pigs," Connie snorted. "Not that I have anything against bacon but I don't know how to butcher one either. Still, it's a thought. But I also found a notice about puppies."

"Puppies?" I asked. I couldn't actually see my eyebrows of course, but I was sure they had gone up.

"Yeah," she looked up, grinning. "I had the thought that if things get that bad, it wouldn't hurt to have a good dog. And if they don't we'll still have a good guard dog, right?"

Okay, at this point a number of things went through my mind. Getting a dog, *together*, was one of those things that couples did. I didn't know if we officially represented a couple or not, but I did *so* love the idea. Second, she spoke as if we would still be. . .whatever we were, even if the world *wasn't* ending. Third, I really liked all the 'we' she was using in her sentences. All of which led me to say;

"Whatever you want." She beamed at me and my knees went a little watery, but I maintained. Couldn't look unmanly in front of Pimply after all. Connie finished making notes and we departed.

We had only been inside for a few minutes, five at most, but I swear things looked worse in just that short a time.

Connie sat in the truck and made a few calls, finding a half-dozen chickens and a rooster for practically nothing. I had eased us into traffic and we were already going the right direction so we were good on that score, but I pulled into the Tractor Supply parking lot as we headed out of town.

"What are we doing?" Connie asked.

"We need a pet taxi or something to put the chickens in," I shrugged. "And we need to look and see if there's some kind of chicken house or something. And maybe a book on raising chickens. I got nothing on that score."

"True," she nodded and climbed down. It took several minutes but soon enough we had what we needed and Connie had picked up some puppy food and a few toys, along with the vaccinations she would need. Apparently even a people doctor could get the stronger meds usually reserved for vets. Or maybe it was just a guy trying to impress a great looking woman, I didn't know. I did know how he felt, though.

Fifteen minutes later we were back on the road, first stop the chicken place. The elderly couple had more than they could say grace over and were slowly weeding down their livestock.

"Nothin' wrong with 'em," the elderly farmer assured me. "Just don't need 'em no more. Good layers and they'll raise if'n you want chicks later on." I nodded as if all that made sense to me. And it did sort of. Connie had bought a book at Tractor Supply so I figured I could get the hang of it. Probably.

We loaded the birds into the oversize pet taxi and placed it in back of the truck, the birds clucking nonstop. We loaded ourselves up and headed for the 'puppy place'. A couple with three Labrador Retriever pups left, two males and one female. It was a fairly quick trip since every car in a twenty mile radius seemed to be crammed into town at the moment.

We were no more out of the truck than here came three bundles of fur running at top speed to see who we were. An older, larger version trailed after them, watching us carefully and barking until someone came to the door.

Connie was *oohing* and *ahhing* over all the pups, but one in particular was determined to get her attention, a little chocolate colored male that grabbed the laces on one of her shoes and pulled it, untying her shoe. She laughed as she retied the knot while her new admirer rolled on the ground in front of her, yapping madly.

They were all about eight weeks old and looked good to me. The owner had a shot record for them, and papers. They weren't free, or even cheap, but the pedigree looked pretty good. I watched and waited until Connie decided that Shoe Lace was going to be the one. I paid the man for him and accepted the papers while she busied herself hugging her new friend. Shaking my head I held the struggling, wiggling bundle of hair as Connie climbed back into the truck and then handed him off. The other two, sensing they were losing their brother, rared up on my legs, I guess trying to get me to load them up as well. The owner shooed them on their way and soon we were on the road once more, Connie playing with her new puppy.

"Thank you, Drake," she said softly and I glanced her way to see her looking intently at me.

"You're welcome," I nodded. "He's a cute little fella," I added.

"He's adorable," she agreed happily. Hey, if she was happy, so was I. You can go ahead and think what you want, but by then I was long past the 'lust' stage of my attraction to Connie Kane. At the very least I was infatuated. Honestly I think I was already completely in love with her at that point.

Like it or not we had to go back through town to get home, so we brainstormed as we made our way through traffic. Nothing came to mind though, and we had a chicken house to assemble and a puppy to play with and zombies to watch for so we headed home.

Connie took care of the playing with the puppy while I assembled the chicken house. Since the yard was fenced we could release the chickens to roam free so long as we watched the dog. As they pecked their way across the yard I realized that the chickens would serve to help keep down the tick and flea population as well, an added benefit that I hadn't considered. Not a bad add-on to the eggs and meat angle I thought.

Once all that was finished it was starting to head into late afternoon and I admit I was getting hungry.

"You want to go out?" I asked Connie as we finally managed to herd the last of the chickens into the small enclosure. Water and feed were waiting for them inside so it wasn't that difficult, really.

"You think we should?" she asked, still playing with the puppy.

"What are you going to call him?" I asked instead of answering. "He needs a name."

"I don't know," she admitted, looking at him again. "Choc? Count Chocula?" I laughed aloud at that as she grinned sheepishly.

"Better than Boo Berry," I told her, and that got a laugh from her. "I don't know.

He's rambunctious, that's for sure," I added as the pup squirmed in her arms, trying to turn where he could lick her. I knew how he felt. (If I wasn't going to hell before, I am now).

"Ram," she nodded firmly. "Short for rambunctious. I like it. A good strong name for our protector," she cooed at him and was rewarded with a bunch of sloppy kisses. I sighed. *Oh to be a dog.*

"Well, Ram it is," I nodded. "As to going out, there's no reason we can't if you want to. We were supposed to have a date tonight after all," I added.

"Okay," she nodded. "I'd like to. No way to know how many more chances we might have and I admit I was looking forward to it," she gave me a bright smile that would have melted iron. I wasn't going to make it. Just was not. Going. To make it.

"Well, let me get cleaned up. We can get 'Ram' settled in the garage for now and then head out."

"I don't want him to live in the garage," Connie frowned.

"I didn't say he'd live there," I held up my hands in self-defense. "Just stay there while we're out. He's not house-broken or anything so he'd make a mess. He can stay inside with us if he wants. Don't forget he's used to being outside." She nodded, mollified. I didn't figure he'd want to be separated from her for long, anyway. And I knew exactly how he felt, too.

I went inside and ran through the shower. Connie did the same and while she was getting ready I made 'Ram' comfortable on a bed we'd gotten him at Tractor Supply, showing him a puppy pad that I knew he'd never use. I fixed him a bowl of water and then put a can of meaty puppy food in the other bowl we'd gotten for him. He gobbled it down as if he hadn't eaten since he'd been weaned. Growing dog and all that, I guess.

Before he was finished Connie was there with us, laughing at his grunting sounds while he ate. He was a cute little thing. I knew he'd grow pretty quick with good food and care, but for now he was just about the size of a teddy bear and cuter.

Leaving him there we headed out on our 'date'. Connie suggested using her car but after what we'd seen in town that day I shook my head. I had taken Big Baby out of storage to use in times like this. No sense not using her. Connie grumbled slightly at having to climb up the ladder but better safe than sorry. And getting to help her climb aboard was a treat all in itself.

Hey, you take life's pleasures where you find them, man.

CHAPTER SEVEN

We rolled into town just at sundown. Yes, I know how that sounds but I'd already written it down. Anyway, town had calmed some but it really was still a madhouse. It seemed that several stores were completely sold out of most everything already judging by the signs in several store windows. It was also possible that those owners were simply saving whatever was left for their own families and if they were I didn't blame them.

But you could bet that others would.

"I don't know about this, Drake," Connie's voice broke into my thoughts. "I thought maybe things would have settled down by now," she admitted.

"So did I," I agreed. "If places are already running out of stuff then people are going to start going nutty soon."

"I thought of that," she nodded absently. "I just wish I had thought of it *before* we left the house."

"Well, we can always go back," I shrugged. "Up to you. We can order a pizza if you want and take it home. Watch a movie or something." She grinned at me when I said 'or something', but I swear I meant play cards or a board game, 'something' like that. I swear I did. Cross my heart.

"Okay," she nodded. "Since we're here, we might see about getting a better supply of dog food," she suggested. "I only got a little bit since I wasn't sure we'd even get him."

"Works for me," I nodded. "Call. . .Papa John's?" I asked. She nodded and took out her cell phone. She punched in the number while I drove. After almost a minute I noticed that she wasn't speaking and glanced at her. She was frowning, looking at her phone.

"I don't have a signal?" she looked and sounded puzzled and for good reason. Right here in town there should have been a signal with no problem. I took my phone and handed it to her.

"Try mine." She took it and looked at the screen then shook her head.

"Nothing." A little icy tingle went up my spine at that. There was no reason at all for us not to have a signal. Jammed circuits I could understand and even expect considering what we'd heard on the television earlier. But no signal? No, that was wrong.

"What do we do?" she asked, and I could tell she was thinking the same thing I was.

"We'll stop, order the pizza, get the dog food, go pick up the pizza, and go home," I said firmly. She nodded but said nothing. Wasn't really anything to say, anyway.

We rolled up to the pizza place and I have to admit I was surprised to see it open. Rather than go inside I pulled around to the pickup window. The girl at the window looked wide-eyed at the sight of Big Baby and cautiously opened the window.

"Hi," I smiled trying to put her at ease. "We tried to call an order in but couldn't get a signal," I held up my phone. "Can I place an order and then come pick it up after I run an errand?"

"Sure," she nodded, blond ponytail waving as she did. Her name tag said her name was Heather and I figured she was about sixteen or seventeen maybe, but nowadays it was hard to tell. For all I knew she was twenty-five. Regardless, she took our order. We decided to get more than one since it really was looking like getting more might be a problem. I paid in advance and told her to keep the change, maybe four dollars. I thought that might help make sure that our pizza got done as soon as possible. She smiled brightly at the 'tip' and promised our pizza would be ready in about thirty minutes.

"We're really busy tonight to be honest," she admitted. "Even for Saturday."

"I understand," I told her and I really did. Connie and I weren't the only people having what might be our last slice of civilization. We left Heather to make our pizza while we headed back to get the dog food. We had some better luck since it seemed no one was worried about getting any farm supplies at the moment. We bought maybe three hundred pounds of dog food and a good supply of treats. The bill was hefty to say the least but assuming the worse happened, Ram would eat. If it didn't happen I wouldn't have to buy dog food for a good while. Win-win, right?

It took maybe twenty-five minutes to get there, get the stuff and get loaded. I noticed right at the last minute three five gallon gas cans and added them to the till. When we left I went straight back to the Co-op where, as I suspected, there was no line for the pumps. Their fuel is always a bit higher than most places. Once more I filled Baby and then the three new cans. Another fifteen gallons of gas for the end of the world.

Connie stayed in the truck while I worked the pump, keeping watch. It seemed ridiculous but things were already out of hand and they could only get worse. I hurried as much as I could and was glad to get back into the truck. I was starting to think we should have stayed at home.

It was a silent ride back to Papa John's and Heather to get the pizza. Heather remembered us and smiled again as she passed three pizzas and two boxes of bread sticks through the window. As I took the last box I glanced over her shoulder as the door opened in their lobby and a very shady looking individual walked inside. Tall, too skinny with a head that was all but shaved, tattoos that had never been done in a legitimate tattoo place and looking about as jumpy as a cat in a room full of rocking chairs.

If this guy wasn't a meth-head I'd eat Baby's bumper.

"Call 911," I told Connie softly, never taking my eyes off Methie.

"What?"

"Call 911, right now," I repeated. "This guy's about to rob them."

"Drake, there's still no signal," she reminded me. Shit. *Shit shit shit*! I pulled Baby forward far enough to get the door open and stopped again.

"What are you doing?" Connie asked.

"I can't let him kill that kid," I told her flatly. "He's wired to the gills, Connie. Keep trying to get a signal and get your pistol out." I opened the door and started to climb down but Connie grabbed my arm. I turned, expecting some kind of opposition or argument, but instead she had moved to the middle of the seat and suddenly kissed me soundly, right on the mouth.

Okay, I have to stop here and admit to you that this was not how I envisioned that happening. Not here in the friggin' Papa John's parking lot. Know what I mean? That being said it was glorious. Ab-so-fucking-lutely *glorious*. I could lie and say that I was so surprised that I froze, but it would be a lie. Well okay I did *sort* of freeze for *just* a second, but then I did what any red blooded American boy would have done in that same situation.

I kissed her back. Soundly.

After what seemed like days she pulled away, face flushed and breathing hard.

"You come back," was all she said. Still slightly stunned, I nodded dumbly and got out. What was I getting out for? I suddenly couldn't remember what I'd been about to. . .oh, robbery. Meth-head. Got it. I drew my pistol, holding it down beside my leg as I walked to the door. I got there just as

Methie pulled a revolver from his pants and pointed it at Heather. Cute girl Heather, and polite. No way I could let this happen.

She saw me in the door and I raised my hand, palm down, then acted as if I was pushing something down. *Get down.* I hoped she got it.

She got it. Heather hit the floor in a flash as I opened the door. The door that had a damn bell on it to announce that a customer had entered the store. Which I would have *known* had I got *out of the truck* to order the damn pizza.

Methie whirled around at the sound of the bell since it was right above the door behind him. Seeing the revolver coming my way I didn't hesitate. I'm not a cop so I didn't have to yell 'halt' or 'freeze' or any of that cop-shit. Instead I shot Methie right in the face.

Now, I'll admit that I was not *aiming* at his face. I was in face aiming at his *chest.* How I hit him in the face I cannot explain. He was moving so maybe that was it. I was also *scared shitless* which might also explain it. What had looked like the right thing to do when I started out had just turned into an 'oh-shit' situation in about three seconds.

You know how in the movies they sometimes show the bad guy, or the good guy comes to that, getting shot in slow motion? Time seems to slow down and all that? That's what it seemed like to me for just about five seconds.

My forty-five boomed inside the small store and my ears were ringing before the empty casing hit the floor. I only fired the one time but it was more than enough. Have you ever seen what a forty-five caliber hollow-point does to a human head? I hadn't either until right then.

I'd say it was spectacular but that just seems wrong somehow. I'll spare you the gory details except to say that Methie's head exploded like a cantaloupe. It was that bad. Blood and brains went everywhere behind him. . . .

Okay that's not really sparing you, is it. Anyway, Methie was dead long before he hit the ground. Not to be melodramatic about it but. . .well, in technical terms he had just suffered massive head trauma. He was as dead as George Washington right there in the floor of the Papa John's pizza parlor.

As a technical question, is a place that is pick-up and delivery only still considered a parlor? I mean if there's no tables and stuff, you just pick the food up and go home with it? I don't know either.

"You can get up now," I called out, louder probably than I needed to but I was still about half deaf from the gunshot. I saw a hand appear from behind the counter, gripping it hard. Heather soon followed, dragging herself off the floor her eyes now much wider than when Baby had pulled into the drive-through window. She looked at me and then down at Dead Methie, then back up at me.

"Is. . .is he dead?" she asked hesitantly.

"Most definitely," I nodded. I felt my hands starting to shake about then and very carefully holstered my pistol. I used my hands to scrub my face and then tried to shake the ringing out of my ears. Ever notice how we do that? Think we can *shake* that ringing away? It doesn't work. Doesn't really hurt anything, but it doesn't help, either.

I had never shot anyone before. Never had to, you know? I hadn't planned on shooting Methie, either. I had it in my mind to just hold him at gunpoint until the police got there and then let them take him. Honest citizen doing his civic duty, right?

That damn bell. It had given me away and made Methie turn the gun on me. I was okay with that since it took the gun off those two teenagers working the pizza place, but I had screwed up by the numbers. I shook that away and looked at Heather.

"Call 911?" I asked. She nodded mutely and picked up the phone. She stood there a second and then hit the toggle to try and get a dial tone. She looked up at me, face puzzled.

"There's no dial tone," she said evenly. "I don't understand. It was working just a few minutes ago." She was going into shock it looked like. I tried to remember what you had to do to treat shock victims. Keep them elevated? No, that wasn't right. Warm? It was pretty warm in here already. Damn it I *know* there was something about this in my first aid class. . . .

"Drake are you okay?" I turned to see Connie standing behind me, gun in hand. She looked at Methie, made a frownie face and then looked back to me.

"I said are you okay?" she demanded a little more urgently and I nodded.

"I think Heather is in shock, maybe," I told her. Connie nodded and put her own gun away, moving to where Heather The Pizza girl was starting to shake a little, tears tracking down her face. A short teenage boy with wild looking hair and a scraggly beard was peering out from behind a rack used to hold pizzas ready for pickup.

"Hey kid!" I shouted and he cringed, looking like he was ready to bolt. I hadn't mean to shout I just still couldn't hear too good.

"It's okay," I tried to lower my voice. "See if you can get the phone to work and call 911, okay? I think Heather may need an ambulance and we definitely need the cops." He nodded his head so rapid and jerkily that if I hadn't just killed someone it would have been funny. He went to a phone in back of the little store and tried to place a call. I saw him frown and punch the buttons again. After three tries he gave up and walked to the counter. His name tag said Rick.

"Mister, the phone's not working," Rick said, trying not to look at Methie and trying to act calm in front of Heather. *Good kid* I decided.

"Look, you got a car?" I asked and he nodded again.

"Drive to City Hall and tell the dispatcher what happened, will you? And please tell them not to come in shooting because I'm honest to God the good guy here. Please?"

"I will," Rick promised solemnly. He took three steps and then stopped to look at me again.

"Uh, I'm not supposed to leave the store," he said as if he'd just thought of it. He probably had, come to think of it.

"I don't think that 'll matter tonight," I promised him. "I think you're closed for the night, Rick," I added, looking down at Methie.

"Oh. Yeah." With that Rick was out the door and gone. I looked at Connie who was still with Heather. She nodded her head letting me know that Heather was okay, or at least uninjured. I then did something I rarely ever do. *Ever.*

I apologized.

"Heather," I said, trying to keep my voice even. I still couldn't hear that well. She looked at me.

"Heather, I'm really sorry about this," I said softly. "I didn't mean for that to happen. I just wanted to make sure he didn't hurt you two."

"Thank you," she said softly. "I saw him earlier, standing outside," she added, though she very carefully didn't look at Methie. "I thought he was just creepy, you know? Maybe waiting for me to come outside after work? We always call the police for an escort when we close so I didn't call them about him before. I wish I had, now."

So did I, but it wouldn't do to say that.

"Don't worry about that now," I said instead, shaking my head. "It's not your fault. This guy came in here to rob you and he might have hurt both of you doing it. I still wouldn't have made you see that if I could have helped it."

"Better than the alternative," she shrugged and that kinda surprised me. Heather was apparently not just another blonde. (If you're a blonde don't take that personal. There's a girl at my office that's. . . well, you don't care about that.) This girl was smarter than the average pizza cashier it seemed.

I heard a siren about then and looked outside. I couldn't see the car yet but blue strobes were reflecting off anything that would catch a light. I walked to the bench along the wall and sat down. Better to look non-threatening so that some over-eager little JBT didn't shoot me on sight.

Okay, that wasn't fair. Our city police were mostly good guys as far as I knew and a few were even members of our gun club. Still, better safe than sorry, right? Three patrol cars screeched to a halt in front of the store and four officers got out, guns in hand. One came to the door and opened it, seeing Connie and Heather standing behind the counter and I caught my first break of the night. I knew the guy.

"Harold, don't shoot us," I said calmly and he turned to face me. He was all business until he saw me and relaxed a bit.

"Drake?" Harold Falter's eyes shot up. "What the hell, man?"

"Methie," I pointed to the dead guy, "tried to rob this place a few minutes ago. We tried to call 911 but we couldn't get a signal. He had a gun," I pointed to the revolver lying on the floor next to Methie. "I was gonna to try and get the drop on him because we couldn't get through to you guys, but the damn door bell rang and he turned the gun on me. Better than the kids," I shrugged. Harold holstered his gun and keyed his radio.

"Go ahead and send the wagon," he ordered. "Scene secure." In seconds an ambulance rolled into the lot.

"I really don't think they can help him," I told Harold. He snorted at my statement of obviousness.

"For the girl," he nodded to Heather. "You and Connie?" he asked, and I nodded.

"Just wanted a pizza before the zombies hit, you know?" I said helplessly. "Fuckin' meth-head."

"It's all right, Drake," Harold told me, sitting down beside me. "Never had to do this before I take it?"

"No reason to," I nodded. I have to admit that I was taking this pretty well. I'd never really thought of myself as a killer, you know? But I was now.

"This won't mean much right now," Harold said gently, "but you did a good thing, bro. Don't sweat it."

"I suppose you'll wanna take me to jail?" I asked and I might have tensed just a bit. I was not going to spend the start of the zombie apocalypse in jail. Not even for

Harold. I looked up as two more officers came inside, one with his gun still out.

"Normally, yeah," Harold admitted. "Tonight is anything but normal, though. The world's coming to an end, you know?" he grinned slightly and I couldn't help but snort as I nodded.

"Look, I'm supposed to take your gun and log it as evidence, but. . .I think you'll need it before long." He paused and looked at the other two cops. Both of whom shrugged as if to say 'whatever you think'.

"Let one of these guys get your statement, and Connie's, and then you guys get outta here," Harold said suddenly. "This whole night has been crazy and it's just getting worse. We've got too much going to hold someone like you. Besides I know where to find you," he grinned. Harold Falter had drank many a beer on my couch watching college football.

"Yeah, you know where to find me," I agreed. Harold slapped me on the shoulder and then got to his feet. One of his men came and sat down beside me with a clipboard as the EMTs moved in. They spared a glance for Methie and then went to check on Heather. I heard Connie telling them what she had observed, then Harold was talking to her.

"Name?" the officer who sat down beside me asked.

"I don't know his name," I admitted. "Never seen him before."

"I meant your name, sir," he said gently and I felt stupid. Of course he meant my name.

"Sorry," I told him and he waved it off as unimportant.

"Shelton Drake," I told him. "Everyone just calls me Drake." I spent probably the next twenty minutes going over what had happened with Officer. . .you know, I don't know his name. I didn't think to ask and he didn't offer and I don't know who he was. Ain't that a hell of a thing? You'd think I'd remember the guy who talked to me about blowing someone's head off, wouldn't you?

Anyway, after twenty or so minutes of that he finally stood up. Officer I Don't Know looked down at me and smiled just a little.

"Between you and me," he said softly, "you did the town a favor. This guy is. . .was, bad news. A predator, if you know what I mean. If what Heather said was accurate, he would probably have hurt her if not killed her outright. Rick too. I know that might not help much now, but remember it. You're free to go Mister Drake. Just don't leave town."

I looked up at him. Did he really just say that? Then I saw him smile and chuckled a little. This guy wasn't very old but seemed to know just how to help someone move along.

"I've always wanted to say that," he confided with a wink. "Go home, sir. Be safe." With that he was gone, out the door and to another call I'd guess. I hope he made it. He was a good guy. Harold was the last to leave, waiting as the M.E. van pulled in to retrieve Methie. I never did ask what his name was. Don't really care to be honest. Fuckin' meth-head.

"Drake, time for you to go home bro," Harold told me. "It's all right, man. If the world doesn't end we'll probably have to have a Coroner's Inquest, but. . .I wouldn't hold my breath," he admitted.

"That bad?" I asked. He looked around as if to see if anyone was listening then turned back to me, his face hard.

"Lying bastards waited until whatever this thing is was in the States before saying anything. I don't know if it will get out or not but. . .the news we're getting is bad. All of it. That's why nobody gives a shit about a dead meth-head. One less zombie to kill later."

"Zombie," I repeated the word.

"No one's callin 'em that," Harold admitted. "But I've seen the videos. Some of them anyway. New York, Boston, Baltimore and D.C. all have reported cases. There's unconfirmed reports out of Atlanta, Jacksonville and Miami. All east coast International Airports. All flight from Europe. If they had just shut down the incoming we might have been all right." He stopped suddenly shaking his head angrily.

"Anyway, the last report I saw, about an hour-and-a-half ago, said the situation in New York was and I quote, 'grave'.

'Serious' was the word for the others. Apparently containment is lost. So you watch yourself."

"Harold, if things get too bad what are you going to do?" I asked him suddenly. He took a deep breath and let it out slowly.

"I ain't got that far," he admitted finally. "I need to hang in as long as I can I guess. I took an oath. Can't very well just run out on that, can I?" he grinned sourly.

"Harold, if you need anything, or a place to go when the shit gets deep, remember you know where I am," I told him. This man was my friend and had just done me a great big fat favor. No way was I going to leave him hanging.

"I appreciate that D. I really do. And I'll remember. Now get your fine ass woman and get the hell out of here while you still can. Be safe." I shook his hand and waved for Connie to join me. She hugged Heather the Pizza girl and met me at the door.

"Are you okay?" she asked, worry in her eyes. Her concern made my heart flutter a bit. I nodded, taking her hand. She squeezed my hand and we headed for Baby.

I helped her inside the driver's door and then crawled in behind her. It was all my legs would do to get me in the cab.

"Let's go home, Drake," Connie said gently. She had moved over only enough to let me get inside and sat beside me all the way to the house. I didn't speak. I really didn't have anything to say to be honest. There was only one thing that was bothering me at the moment.

That it *hadn't* bothered me to kill Methie. I mean, on the face of it, why should it, right? Nominally he was a human being, but he was also a piece of shit. A predator Officer I Don't Know had called him. Son-of-a-bitch was probably going for a two-fer in robbing the place and hurting Heather The Pizza Girl (I need to stop calling her that don't I?). And he would have shot me just for walking inside.

World was better off without him, right? Like Harold had said, one less Zombie to kill when the time came, right?

"Drake are you all right?" Connie's soft questions cut into that train of thought.

"I'm fine," I told her, meaning it. "I wish it hadn't happened," I admitted, glancing at her with a half-ass smile. "Kinda ruined our evening. Sorry."

"Shut up," she said gently and kissed me lightly. "That was a brave thing you did back there. He would have hurt Heather if not killed her. Her and Rick both. You saved them, Drake."

"Yeah, big hero," I snorted. "All I did was shoot a thug. In front of a teen-age girl who'll probably need years of therapy. Assuming she doesn't get eaten by zombies of course," I just *had* to add.

"Drake I'm not listening to that shit," she said more forcefully. "Harold told me that guy was well known to them and he's attacked more than one young woman. He's always been able to intimidate them into not pressing charges so he's gotten away with it until tonight."

"Most men would have driven away and then maybe, *maybe* gone to City Hall and reported it then gone home to eat pizza. Do you remember what you said when you started to get out of the truck?" she asked. I looked at here for a second, probably with a dumb look on my face. Hell all I could remember was her kissing me. *That* I would remember as long as I lived.

"You said, and I quote, 'I can't let him kill that kid'. Exact words. You never thought about your own safety. *That* I'm not too thrilled over to be honest," she frowned. "But you walked right in there because of those two teenagers. I'm pretty sure Heather has a little hero crush on you already," she teased gently and I snorted again.

"I'm taken," I said without thinking and she leaned against me.

"You damn sure are," she whispered into my ear, her voice husky. My spine tingled at that along with a few other things as well.

My head was still spinning when I pulled into the yard and closed the gate behind me. Ram was barking his little head off in the garage, happy to see his mommy. We carried the now cold pizza into the house and I took a quick shower while Connie played with Ram and cleaned up after him. I came into the kitchen still drying my hair. Connie had the pizza heating in the oven and went to shower and change, telling me to watch the pizza.

I sat down at the table and did just that. While I sat there I played the events over one more time and realized there really wasn't anything I could have done different. As I thought back to my conversation with Harold I remembered what he'd said about some cases already being in the States. I got up and went to get my laptop, setting it on the kitchen table. Soon I was perusing news sites looking for new information.

There was a lot of newly posted stories but so far the media was downplaying the cases of the 'virus' already present in the States. True, they reported the 'incidents', but made no effort to challenge the official story. They took it at face value and passed it on to Joe Six-pack without even trying to investigate.

"What are you looking at?" Connie asked as she came back into the kitchen. She smelled like roses and looked even better. I just showed her the screen as I flipped through the pages from the large cities news stations.

"Harold told me things were pretty bad already," I informed her as she took the pizza from the oven. "Says that the Feds sat on things until the virus was already loose. He doesn't know if they can contain it now. There are reports of outbreaks in New York, D.C., Baltimore, Boston, Atlanta, Jacksonville and Miami. He noted they were all eastern International Airports. All with flights direct from Europe."

"So it's already here," she said stoically and I nodded.

"'Fraid so." I shut the laptop and sat there. Connie was back and forth for a few moments and then suddenly she was standing right in front of me.

"All right, mister," she said sternly. "You owe me a movie." She held out her hand and I couldn't help but laugh a little. I let her pull me out of my chair and lead me to the den where she already had a movie playing. We ate a little pizza while we watched Iron Man kill terrorists, then ate some more while we watched Paul Bettany kill vampires. By the time that one was over Connie was almost in my lap, kissing gently on my ear. I don't recall if Bettany killed the last vamp or not if you know what I mean.

Before I realized what was happening we were in Connie's room, kissing pretty hotly. As things progressed I realized that I was about to see my dream girl completely naked and ready for some serious contact sports if you get my meaning.

"Wait," I heard someone say and was shocked, *shocked* I tell you, to realize it was me. (I can say now that I had lost my fucking mind. There's no other explanation.) It dawned on me that she might be doing this because of what had happened. Because she thought it would distract me from killing Methie. (Connie Kane naked in my bed, hell in *any* bed, would distract me from a dinosaur attack. Just thought I'd throw that in there). I was afraid she was doing this just to comfort me. The thought was priceless, but. . .it would be dishonest to take advantage of her like that. As bad as I wanted what she was obviously offering I just couldn't take advantage. And I *really* wanted to take advantage I'm telling you right now. I've never had a lot of willpower and it was strained to the breaking point along with some other things.

"What?" she asked a little breathlessly.

"Connie, you know I want. . .I mean but not because -" she cut me off with another kiss, this one so deep that I think she examined my tonsils while she was at it.

"It's not," she whispered huskily. "Got nothing to do with it. Now stop talking."

I stopped talking.

CHAPTER EIGHT

I woke up the next morning to a sun brightened room and realized that I had slept later than I had in. . .well, I don't know how long. There was an entirely pleasant pressure on my chest and I had a face full of wonderful smelling black hair.

Holy shit, Connie was laying on top of me *naked as the day she was born*. The events of the night before came back to me then and I know, I just *know*, that a stupid smile made its way across my face. I had made it with my dream girl.

I will admit to you that my very first thought after that was that I needed to find a preacher and marry her. I'm sure that sounds corny and I don't really care. All I could think of at that moment was that I wanted this to last forever. I wanted her as a part of my life for the *rest* of my life, however long that might be.

The second thought was that I wanted that to be a very long time, which meant I had to make sure that we stayed safe. I knew at that moment that I would give my life to keep her safe.

My next thought was that I had to pee so bad my bladder was about to burst.

Ruined the moment, didn't I? Sorry about that, but it was true. I hated the thought of disturbing her she looked so peaceful and beautiful lying there, but I really, *really* had to pee. I very carefully eased out from beneath her and then out of the room to my own bathroom, gently closing her door behind me. I made my way into my own bath and relieved that pressure, then took a shower. Once dressed I made my way to the kitchen and started some coffee, put some biscuits in the oven and some sausage patties in a skillet. That done I got my laptop and turned on the television to see what shape the world was in this fine and wonderful Sunday morning.

I can't really say I was surprised to see fires burning out of control in most of the major cities. Looting was widespread in the cities that Harold had mentioned as having lost 'containment' the night before and believe it or not there were protesters out in force in many of those same cities. I have no idea what exactly they were protesting and didn't bother to check to be honest. Idiots. All they were doing was making it easier for the virus to be spread.

The smell of my breakfast cooking pulled me away from the tube as I made my way back to the kitchen. I used my tablet to scroll through various news pages looking for anything I didn't already know. There wasn't much other than reports of 'disturbances' in some new areas. None near us at the moment, at least not any zombie or virus related disturbances. The city itself was having its share of problems with looting and such but that wasn't zombies. Well, not *those* zombies anyway.

I probably should have mentioned that I live in a suburb of a much larger city. Well, that's not entirely accurate. I live just across a county line from a major metropolitan area. Just twenty minutes from me was a city of over a million people. My little suburb community had about twenty thousand total I'd guess. I hadn't even considered the impact that the metro area was having on our own little slice of heaven last night but it was entirely probable that Harold and his partners were having so much action because of some metro incursions.

That made me think of Harold and I hoped he was okay. If the phones were working later I'd try to call him maybe.

I heard water running and figured Connie was in the shower. I admit I had to smile again at the thought of her. I'm sure that most of you are snorting at me about that but that's fine. It just means that you've never had a dream come true and I feel sorry for you. No, seriously. I hope you get at least one dream that comes true. It's magnificent.

As everything else finished up I scrambled some eggs and had breakfast on the table as my lovely doctor came into the kitchen wearing a tee shirt and pair of boy shorts. Oh man, I do love those boy shorts.

I had a moment's trepidation as she walked in, wondering if last night was going to make this morning awkward or uncomfortable. I hoped not because I really didn't know how I'd handle that to be honest. I was sure that my heart would break in two if she told me that she regretted. . . .

She walked straight to me and kissed me. I mean like she meant it, know what I mean? And I kissed her back, too. When we broke apart she smiled the sexiest damn smile I have ever seen.

"Morning cowboy," she breathed. God she smelled wonderful.

"Morning ma'am," I smiled back. "How are you this morning?" Damn it, that wasn't what I meant to ask. I might as well have asked her 'how was it?'.

"I'm wonderful," she literally purred and I felt a stirring somewhere south of the Mason Dixon line but fought it down. "How 'bout you?" she asked me, leaning into me and resting her head on my shoulder. I was in heaven. Might not be dead yet but was definitely in my version of heaven.

"I slept like a baby," I admitted. "I have made you breakfast, my lady," I added and pulled a seat out for her. She sat down, laughing lightly. I was so grateful for the fact that things not only weren't awkward but were, in fact, just *dandy.*

"How are you, really?" she asked more seriously as she fixed a plate.

"I'm really fine," I told her, knowing what she meant. "I still hate it happened, but honestly that's more because of the girl having to see it. He needed killing," I shrugged. "If I'd had my druthers it wouldn't have been me that done it, but I literally didn't lose any sleep over it," I grinned.

"What *did* you lose sleep over?" she asked mischievously.

"Over you of course," I answered at once. Yeah, yeah, I know you're making a gag motion right now but that's fine. Help yourself. I seriously couldn't have cared less at that moment and still don't.

"I assume you've already checked the news?" she asked as she took a bite of egg. "Oh, that's good," she added, chewing slowly. Man anything she did was just. . .damn. Just damn.

"Yeah. City's having a lot of trouble this morning. Protests and looting and all that."

"Protests?" Connie looked shocked. "About what?"

"I didn't check to be honest," I admitted. "I mean it's just stupid to be out like that in groups, out in the open. Just makes it easier for the virus to spread wouldn't you think?"

"Depends on how it spreads," she shrugged and even *that* was sensual. I'm stopping, I'm *stopping*.

"If it's airborne, then yeah it's a problem," she continued. "Last news we had was that it was strictly fluid transfer, but it seems that we might have been lied to at least some yesterday so I have to take that with a grain of salt."

"Well, if it's really zombies then I guess the movie thing is holding true for the moment," I said. "If it's a true virus though, I remember you saying that it could mutate. Or did Dumbo the Clown say that?" I frowned. I couldn't remember.

"Any true virus can mutate," Connie nodded. "Since this one at least started as a fluid transfer virus I'm assuming it's blood borne, but that is an assumption. It's entirely possible that once someone is infected that any body fluid can pass the virus. Sooner or later an infected patient's body chemistry may alter the virus into something aerosol, from which point on the virus will be able to spread through the air."

"How's that work, exactly?" I asked.

"Depends on the level of infection and how virulent, or powerful, the virus is," she explained. "If it's very strong, can live outside the host for any length of time over a second or so, then a sneeze is enough to infect anyone near it. Evaporating body fluids or scattered body fluids, say from a gunshot wound," she looked at me pointedly, "can also result in infection. Without details on the virus itself there's just no way to say for sure. The variables are literally endless."

"Well, that's just great," I muttered and she nodded.

"That's why I said yesterday's 'medical' briefing was bullshit," she told me flatly. "Just standard protocol for any infectious disease that's spreading. Come to think of it," she paused briefly, "the bastard might have already known that the virus was airborne. If he did then that would make his warnings to the general public more understandable."

"But all that warning did was create panic," I objected.

"That was going to happen anyway," Connie shrugged. "You can't announce something like that and expect it not to create some kind of panic attack in most of the population. Not everyone is as smart as you are, Drake," she smirked at me just a little as I snorted.

"Yeah, I'm a regular Einstein."

"You cued on this early on," she pointed out. "You didn't have any information that everyone else didn't have access to, just made good decisions made on sound deductive reasoning. Like coming to see me," she added, this time with a full blown smirk of self-satisfaction.

"That's one thing that I will be eternally grateful I thought of," I admitted freely.

"Me too," she rewarded me with a dazzling smile. You know, the kind of smile that convinces a man that he should do pretty much anything the woman smiling at him asks. Like, oh, kill a rampaging lion with his bare hands for instance. The kind of smile that convinces him he *can* kill that lion. And yes, I know how that makes me sound, but I think I already said I don't care. I did say that, didn't I? Yeah, I did.

"Anyway," she continued, "if it wasn't for you, we'd both be in that," she pointed to the tablet laying on the table still showing a picture of panicky people doing. . .well, things panicky people did when they were, panicky. That doesn't sound right does it? Maybe panicking people? Never mind.

"Well, there is that," I nodded. "And we are pretty well set I think. I'm sure there's something we forgot but I can't think what it is at the moment."

"Me either," she admitted. "And that's my point. You put all this together and because you did, we aren't part of the panicking masses that are scrambling around trying to be ready for whatever this might become."

"Well, since we aren't part of that, what should we be doing today?" I asked.

"Absolutely nothing," Connie replied at once. "We've been going almost not-stop since. . .Tuesday? No, Monday. Even without the events of last night, all of them," she added with that sexy smirk she has, "we've earned a day off. I'm technically supposed to see patients tomorrow, too," she added with a frown.

"Still going to?" I asked.

"I should," she temporized. "I mean really I should. All my other appointments were rescheduled for next week after this coming Wednesday, but. . .it's irresponsible for me not to see my patients tomorrow. Assuming any of them come in," she added. "After that, I'll play Tuesday and Wednesday by ear."

"How likely is that?" I asked. "That they'll show up?"

"Depends," she shrugged. "I don't know who was on the schedule. Some may cancel, some may be more determined than ever to get in to see me with things being like they are." She looked up at me. "What are you going to do?"

"I'm off sick," I smirked a little myself. "My office doesn't expect me back until middle of the week, if then. And considering what's going on I don't know how much demand there will be for cyber security over the next few days anyway."

"Is that what you do?" Connie asked with her eyebrows raised and I realized that I'd never told her what I did exactly.

"That is what I do," I nodded. "I travel a lot because of it. My company specializes in protecting databases from hacking and what I call cybernage. Cyber espionage," I explained. "Cybernage is my own little term," I told her proudly.

"You're a hacker?" Connie looked astonished.

"No, I am the *anti*-hacker," I grinned. "I track down hackers and destroy them."

"Uh," she started then stopped.

"Computer wise," I assured her. "I can literally shut down their systems once I turn the hack around on them. I can also trace them for the authorities. Things like that." She stared at me for another few seconds before she giggled slightly. That giggle became a laugh and before I could ask why it became a full-fledged *fit* of laughter.

"Okay, what's so funny about that?" I asked. Not that it wasn't good to hear her laugh, really. It was almost like musical bells. (Shut up!)

"Yo. . .you're a. . .a ne. . .*nerd!*" she wailed again as she finally managed to get the entire sentence out.

"I am not a nerd!" I said indignantly. "I am a highly trained computer forensics and tracking specialist!"

"That's what I said!" Connie was in tears now from laughing so hard. "A nerd!"

Look, I'm *not* a nerd. If I have to have some sort of title then it should be *geek*. Geeks get things done. Nerds live in their mom's basement and play video games.

"I fail to see the humor," I told her. "And I am *not* a nerd." I was trying hard to maintain some dignity here.

"What's so damn funny!" I demanded finally. So much for the dignity thing.

"Oh, my *GOD*!" Connie was literally shaking with laughter. "Of all the things I ever imagined hearing you say, imagined about what you did for a living, being a nerd was *not* on the list!" she busted out laughing again at the look on my face.

"And why is that so hard to believe?" I asked her. "Have I struck you as being in some way too dumb to be a computer expert?"

"No!" she shook her head, trying to stop laughing. "It's just that. . .all this time I've known you at the gun club, known you were a survivalist. . ."

"Prepper," I pointed out in between her laughs.

". . .I just always sort of figured that 'security consultant' meant you were like some kind of quasi-mercenary. Like a high paid ex-military or government agent that had gone freelance. I had n. . .no idea!" she was laughing again.

"Well, sorry to burst your bubble," I shrugged. "But the only work I've ever done for the government was as a contractor back when I was going to school. I worked for different agencies each summer working on computer security systems and helping stop hacking attacks." There was more to it than that, but. . .well, that's all I can say even now, I guess. Be just my luck some asshole of a FED survived and read this and then try to arrest me.

"Does this lower your opinion of me, then?" I asked, suddenly wondering if now that I wasn't some secretive ex-merc type if she would lose interest in me.

"Of course not!" she shot back, laughter suddenly gone. "If anything it just enhances it. Last night's action for a mercenary ex-soldier would have still been something special. For a nerd-boy," she winked slyly, "it's completely fantastic. The way you handled yourself I assumed you had done something like that before."

"No, I hadn't," I assured her, sighing a bit. That seemed to sober her a bit.

"I didn't mean anything in a bad way," she reached out to lay a hand on my arm. "I just seriously always thought you were some kind of para-military type. You just had that kind of air."

"Air?"

"You know. Self-assured, I can handle it, no problem, that kind of thing," she clarified. "Even through all this its been like nothing has phased you. Not that you've allowed to show anyway. You've just gone and done what needed doing."

"Oh," I said, not knowing what else to say. "Well, I've had a lot of different kinds of training over the years. But I'm always outdoors. Shooting, hiking, fishing and hunting. Okay, I guess considering what you knew about me I can see where my profession would surprise you," I admitted after rattling off that list. She nodded.

"Exactly. It's not like I've ever seen you do anything computer related."

"True," I nodded. "Well, at least you're not disappointed," I grinned.

"Oh, no," she shook her head slightly, her voice soft. "No, the one thing I most certainly am not is disappointed." She squeezed my arm at that and I felt a bit better. Oh who am I kidding, I felt like a million bucks hearing that.

"Back to the question at hand," I said, "you are planning on opening your office Monday?" she nodded, albeit reluctantly.

"Barring some kind of Martial Law travel ban, yes. But after Monday I'll have to take it as it comes. I wish I had told Nettie, my receptionist, to cancel everything this week, but. . .maybe tomorrow she can call the others. Assuming the phones are working anyway," she added with a frown.

"Well, I'll take you in and stay with you," I told her. "It's not like I'm doing anything else at the moment. I'm not going into the city and that's where my office is. Nor am I going on the road while all this is playing out. So I'm available," I smiled.

"What about here?" she asked. "Shouldn't you be protecting this place?" I held up my tablet.

"This entire place is wired," I told her. "If someone so much as leans on that fence, let alone tries to get into the house, then I'll know it. I can be here long before they manage to do any damage. Probably before they can get inside," I added, thinking about the storm shutters.

"Well, there's still no reason for you to sit in my office all day. You'll be bored to death!" she exclaimed.

"There is every reason," was my only reply and her blush was a thing to behold. I hoped right then that I would always be able to bring that look to her face.

"That still leaves today," I said as I stood up, taking up the dishes and moving to the sink. "Like you said, we're overdue a rest. I'll need to feed and water the chickens, but otherwise we'll read, watch television and surf the web I guess. Keep up on what's happening."

"Works for me," she hugged me, her arms coming around me in a hug. I turned my head slightly and she kissed my cheek, then walked into the living room. After I watched her go (boy shorts, remember?) I finished the dishes and went to check on the birds. They were fine if a bit loud, but once allowed to roam the yard again they were fine. It occurred to me that I'd have to watch for hawks now. I rarely saw one near the house, but I'd never had anything for them to eat, either.

Once back inside I settled in with Connie to watch the world start to fall apart. I know that sounds melodramatic, but. . .it's pretty much what happened. American newsies had finally seemed to catch on and were now demanding the same answers that their European counterparts had been demanding for days. Our authorities were no more forthcoming than European authorities had been, but our press had a bit more leeway and freedom and they were pissed off at being lied to. Funny thing about the press. They don't mind lying to us, but try lying to them and you are toast.

It really wouldn't matter this time, though. They could roast and toast the politicians all they wanted to but it wouldn't matter. Things were way too far out of hand now and nothing was going to get them under control again. Not without a lot of dead bodies anyway.

As the day progressed things just got worse. By sundown it seemed like the entire world was in a panic. The protesting and rioting was in full swing now and things in city were getting worse as well. Protests and riots had turned to looting had turned to random acts of violence. There were fires burning out of control in several places as firefighters struggled to find enough manpower to be everywhere at once. I assumed that some of them were 'sick', which in this case meant taking care of their own families and the hell with looters and rioters and other kinds of idiots. Hard to blame them, really. Hard to blame any of them.

As night settled in I went and corralled the chickens back into the hen house. I hadn't fed them a great deal that morning so as I threw corn inside the chicken coop they flocked to it. All I had to do was wait and then close the door. That might seem like a normal bit of business to you but remember that I knew nothing about farm animals other than how tasty they were, so for me it was quite an accomplishment.

Ram had spent the day alternating between annoying the shit out of me and playing with Connie and making a mess and sleeping, not always in that order but mostly. I shouldn't say that, I guess, because he wasn't all *that* annoying and he was cute as a button, bouncing around like an over active child. He got into a chair by a window that afternoon and yapped his little ass off at the chickens, clearly wanting to be outside with them. Connie didn't want him outside though and spent a good part of the day trying to get him house-broken and cleaning up after him when it didn't work. Persistence paid off for her though and soon enough he was using the puppy pads more often than not.

We'd have to sooner or later get him used to going outside but for now this was good.

Bedtime snuck up on me to be honest. One minute it's time for supper and I'm cooking, the next Connie is looking down at me while I'm sitting on the couch reading over updated news reports. I looked up at her when she cleared her throat.

"I'm going to bed," she announced. I froze for a moment, knowing I should know something here but not realizing what it was.

"Okay," I settled for saying. "Uh, you want to. . .I mean I can. . .no, what I meant was. . . ." I stammered until she finally took pity on me, laughing.

"Get your ass up," she told me. "I'm moving into your room," she declared as I got to my feet. "I already changed the sheets," she added.

"There was nothing wrong with. . . ." I stopped as she almost-but-not-quite glared at me. Apparently sheets are a big deal to women. Who knew?

I got ready for bed realizing suddenly just how tired I was. I had managed to go the entire day without even thinking about shooting Methie the night before. How 'bout that? Thinking of that made me wonder how Heather and Rick were doing. I hoped they were okay. I really did regret those two kids having to see it.

"Stop thinking about it," Connie told me out of nowhere, kissing my jaw as she passed by me on her way to bed. How she knew what I was thinking I don't know. She's just an amazing woman, that's all.

"I honestly haven't thought about it today," I promised, sliding into bed beside her. "I was just thinking about those two kids, that's all. Hating that they saw it."

"Not your fault," she told me, laying her head on my chest and an arm across my middle. "And they wouldn't be thinking of anything if you hadn't saved them so you think about that instead." I kissed the top of her head and turned out the lamp.

With the world falling apart around me I went to sleep with the woman of my dreams draped across me.

CHAPTER NINE

Turns out that I only got that one night of sleeping more than maybe six hours. I was awake by four-thirty, eyes wide. No way I was going back to sleep.

Connie was still draped across me, neither of us having moved once we went to sleep. I was surprised at that since I usually tossed and turned at night. But I remembered how tired I had suddenly been the night before and figured she might have been too.

I lay there for maybe twenty minutes before carefully sliding from underneath her to get up. I was careful not to wake her, knowing that she had set the clock for six. I used the hallway bathroom to keep the noise down and then walked to the kitchen and started a pot of coffee. As it bubbled and perked it's way to drinkable I turned the TV on to Fox News and turned my computer on.

The news was at least as bad this morning as it had been last night. Riots were still happening everywhere with looting, shooting and random violence in almost every major city, our nearby neighbor being no exception. I looked for any news of a Martial Law declaration or a travel ban but there was none.

I didn't understand that and I still don't. It didn't make sense then and I've seen nothing since to explain it. Why did we not have a travel ban at the very least? Anything to keep the virus from having a way to spread like this? As it was there were no restrictions at all in place. Now I'm the first to admit that those restrictions would probably not have slowed down the rioting and what have you, but it might, *might* have helped in other areas. Since it wasn't done, we'll never know.

I moved to the kitchen with my laptop and used it to watch the latest news stories while I finished breakfast. My lovely doctor was determined to go and see her patients so she needed a good breakfast to start the day and eating breakfast 'out' this morning might be dicey at best. I heard her alarm clock sound and then shut off a moment later. It wasn't long until I heard water running and smiled. She had gone to 'her' bathroom to get ready. Made sense since her things were still there. She'd sooner or later 'move' into my bathroom I was sure, which meant I'd probably be using the hallway bathroom more. I didn't have a problem with that, considering that. . . .

My ruminations on my newly acquired domestic bliss were interrupted when my phone rang. My home phone, no less. *At least we know it's working* I thought as I crossed to check the number. I was surprised to see my office number on the caller identification. I checked my watch. Six-twenty a.m. Strange. I picked up the phone.

"Hello?" I made no attempt to sound asleep. No point in it.

"Drake did you know about this?" My boss/partner Jimmie Melton all but screamed in my ear.

"Uh, I'd have to know what 'this' is before I can answer that," I replied carefully. "And I'm feeling better, yes. Thanks for asking."

"*You know what I mean!*" Melton screamed again. "*You knew all this shit was coming, didn't you?*"

"If by that you are referring to the riots and looting that I just saw on television, then no, James, I did not know. I still don't understand what they're protesting over."

"*I mean the zombies you bastard!*" Melton continued to scream. Oh me. What to do now? Yes I had known. No I had not told anyone else other than Connie and I hadn't planned on telling her. Considering how that had worked out I was still very, *very* glad I ~~hard~~. *Had.* I meant *had.* Swear I did.

"No, I did not," I said evenly. "I knew there was some kind of sickness in Europe. Heard it at the doctor's office in fact. Was supposed to be some kind of avian flu derivative." All of that was *technically* true. Connie had told me all that as I sat in her exam room. "I even got an extra shot because of it, right in the ass," I added. *Also* technically true. I got the shot because I was in a room full of sick people and I would *not* have been there if not for the 'sickness' in Europe. So technically I could say with a clear conscience that I had gotten a shot because of what was happening in Europe at the time.

If lying were an Olympic sport, I'd be a medal contender. If we still had Olympics.

"Drake, I know you keep up with this end-of-the-world shit," Melton sounded a bit calmer now. *"You had to know something."*

"I know just what was on the television, Jimmie," I replied truthfully. "I haven't actually heard the word zombie except from locals and on the web either," I added.

"You've seen them," Melton snorted as if that was all the answer he needed. And it was.

"What can I do?" he asked suddenly.

"Uh, what do you mean?" I asked cautiously.

"There's at least a little time left so what can I do?" he asked again. *"There's got to be a way I can help my family and escape this."*

"Look, I don't know what to tell you James," I admitted. "How much food do you have stored?"

"Not much," he admitted. *"My wife shops week to week and we eat out a lot. There won't be much."*

"You live in the city, don't you?" I temporized.

"Yes. Why?"

"Well, getting out would be the best thing you could do if it's possible," I told him flatly. "Do you guys have any relatives that live outside the city? Maybe on a farm for instance? Somewhere you could make room for yourself and be able to at least grow a garden to feed yourselves if this doesn't stop?"

"Garden?" Melton sounded pissed. *"I'm surrounded by a burning city and you want to talk to me about gardening?"*

"You asked what you could do, James," I replied as Connie came walking into the kitchen. She was Doctor Hottie today and looked gorgeous and I admit my attention might have strayed a bit from. . . .

"Drake are you listening to me?" James Melton's voice brought me back to the phone.

"Look, you asked what you could do," I repeated. "You need to get out of the city if you can and get somewhere off the beaten path. A remote cabin, a family farm, somewhere with family if you can find it. You need to prioritize what you take with you. Drain one car of gas to carry with you and use in the other. Pack food, clothes, shoes, medicines, first-aid supplies, blankets and water. Anything that will carry water fill it from the tap before the services stop."

"What?" Melton was back to screaming. *"Who said anything about the water stopping?"*

"James *look around you*," I was about to scream myself. "Do you seriously think that the city will be able to keep services on in this mess? Hell, the guys who run the plant may not even be able to get to work? What happens if the power dies? No way to clean water, man, or get it to you. You need to find a place with a well if you can."

"Do you have one?" he demanded.

"No, I don't," I admitted. "I tried twice to drill one but. . .nothing. I've got two barrels of water in my garage and. . .well, that's it," I admitted. "If the utilities stop working I'll be forced to drink out of the creek behind my house. Assuming it has water in it, which it doesn't always."

"So what are you doing?" Melton demanded.

"I'm hoping this goes away," I replied, meaning every word. "I don't have any options. No family to go to and no friends living on farms. All I can do is hope it rains regular and that my little garden can feed me."

"Some survivalist you turned out to be," Melton snorted.

"Hey, in my defense I was prepared for an earthquake or something like that. How was I supposed to know there was going to be a zombie outbreak?" I tried to sound a little miffed but basically I was trying to sound like I was on the edge of survival myself and water was my Achilles' Heel. James was right on the cusp of asking me to let him come to my place, and that was out. He and his wife were so snobbish that it hurt to be around them and their two kids were spoiled monsters.

And I flat didn't have enough water for them. Period.

"I should just come out there and make you take care of me," Melton said almost as if he were reading my mind.

"I doubt you could get here, James, and that wouldn't work anyway," I tried to keep my voice even. "I don't have the water. And I can't get it, either."

"Surrounded by guns and nothing to drink," James snorted again and I was starting to get tired of this.

"Surely you or your wife one have some family around," I told him. "Someone further out of the city that you are. A place where you can hole up until this blows over."

"My wife's family have a farm," he admitted. *"But they hate my guts. They'll demand that me and my kids help work their damn farm and I'll be damned if I will."*

"Then you'll probably be hungry, James," I said bluntly. "If this doesn't straighten out, only hard work and toughness will get you through. You may not like it but that's the way it is right now. I'd make good with the in-laws and start teaching my kids to farm, just in case. If all this dries up you can always just come home and tell the folks to shove it and thanks for the memories," I joked, and he laughed a bit.

"Yeah, that might work for a while," he said and I relaxed a little. *"Well, I better get going. Thanks for the info."* The dial tone was the next thing I heard. I hung up the phone, shaking my head as I did so.

"Who was that?" Connie asked, still standing nearby, hands on her hips.

"My boss. Partner. Whatever," I waved the title away. "He wanted to know if I knew about all this. I played a little dumb and maybe lied a little but only by omission," I added, hand raised in virtue.

"I don't care if you lied to *him* just as long as you never lie to *me*," she stressed and kissed me.

"I would die first," I told her without thinking and she blinked at that, eyes wide.

"I would," I shrugged, repeating it. "There's no way I would lie to you. You mean too much to me to risk in any way for any reason." I figured it was truth time here and that was the honest truth if I've ever told it. She almost teared up at my declaration and hugged me tightly for a minute. I finally pried her away and pointed to a chair.

"Take a seat, Doctor Hottie," I said before I thought and she looked at me, startled. Damn my traitorous tongue.

"'Doctor Hottie'?" she asked, eyebrows raised. I blushed a bit and hurried to get her food.

"Slip of the tongue," I told her. "I . . . it's a compliment, promise," I added when the first didn't seem to work.

"Have you ever, and I remind you of the promise you just made to me," she pointed to where I had been standing when I promised not to lie, "*ever*, called me that to anyone else, *ever*?"

"Not that I can think of," I admitted after a moment's thought. "It was just how I always thought of you, that's all. I mean, you're a doctor and you're hotter than the Fourth of July so it just seemed. . .what?" I asked as she started laughing. "What is it?" I demanded.

"Oh, that was priceless!" she wailed in laughter once again at my expense. "You looked like a kid who got caught with his hand in the cookie jar!" I let her laugh for another few seconds before I replied;

"That would be technically accurate," I told her with my own eyebrow raised. That shut her up as her face went beet red and she was suddenly fascinated with her breakfast. She murmured something.

"What?" I asked her and she looked up, smiling sheepishly.

"I said that was a good one, and thank you," she told me.

"For what?" I asked, frowning.

"For playing and laughing and making me smile," she replied. "For helping me forget, even for a few minutes, what may be happening all around us. Thank you." I moved to where she sat and pulled her into a bone crunching hug which she returned just as hard.

"I'll always try to make you smile," I whispered. "And, idiot that I am, I'm sure I'll keep you in stitches for years to come," I added after a few seconds and felt her shake with laughter that she was trying to contain. I released her and stood back looking at her, at which point she burst into laughter again.

"Sit and eat!" I demanded. "We'll have to start in soon." I left her still laughing and eating while I went to get a shower and get dressed. By the time I got back she was all but ready to go and placed Ram in the garage along with his toys and food and water dishes. I checked my inventory and decided I had all I needed. I grabbed my remote and followed her outside.

We exited through the garage with Ram still yapping his indignation at being left behind. I helped Connie into Baby's front seat and then crawled into the driver's seat. I started the engine, and while it warmed a second I held up the remote.

"Observe," I told Connie and pressed a button.

Metal shutters slid into place over each window and door, including the garage doors, slamming shut with enough force that we could hear it over Baby's rumble.

"Holy shit," Connie exclaimed. "That's amazing!"

"Thank you, my Queen," I bowed slightly. "Your Nerd lives to serve."

She was still laughing as we pulled out onto the road and the gate closed behind us.

*****

If town had been a madhouse on Saturday it was an asylum on Monday. I will admit in hindsight we should have expected it to be worse. All I can say is that I had thought perhaps things might have calmed a bit once the initial panic was over. Clearly the initial panic was not over when we got to town Monday morning.

Baby didn't have any trouble negotiating the mess since most sensible people yielded to her in traffic. I managed not to smirk about it but it was difficult. Riding in Big Baby also gave us better vision in traffic since we were so high off the ground.

"I have to admit this monstrosity has its uses," Connie grudgingly complimented. I'm assuming she was just miffed about having the climb in and out. Better a little difficulty than sorry though, right?

"She's awesome," I nodded, weaving in and out of traffic as we headed for her office. There were three wrecks along the way, the drivers having abandoned the cars that were damaged too badly to continue driving. Apparently the police were no less busy today than they had been Saturday night. That couldn't be good.

Despite the traffic issues we made it to Connie's office without any real difficulty. The difficulty started when we got there.

The glass entrance door to her practice was shattered and the picture window in the waiting room was broken.

"Aw, hell," Connie sounded more pissed off than anything. "That's a mess," she sighed. She opened her door but I grabbed her arm before she could step out.

"Calmly now," I warned. "For all we know whoever did it is still in there." I could tell by the look in her eyes that she hadn't thought of that. "We'll check it out together and then see if we can get the police out here," I told her. She nodded and reached into her bag, pulling her pistol. I hit the kill switch on my Baby to prevent anyone stealing her and climbed down, drawing my own pistol. The same one I had used to kill Methie with in fact. That was a sobering thought.

"Let's try not to have to shoot anybody," Connie said as she met me in front of the rig. I nodded, starting to wonder if she could read my mind. I took a deep breath and stepped through the broken door frame, cutting the room with my pistol. The waiting room was empty and there didn't seem to be any damage other than the door and window. The security door to the patient exam and records area was hanging on the bottom hinge.

I nodded to the door and made my way over there, Connie following where she could cover me. That almost sounds like cop shit doesn't it? Truth is this was one of the things we trained for at the club once in a while. Even though we weren't professionals we knew enough to get the job done.

I entered the hallway and reached for the light switch. The lights flared to life in the hallway and Connie groaned at the destruction visible.

"Son-of-a-bitch," she muttered. "What the hell do I pay the alarm company and taxes for?" I agreed but stayed focused. I'd been down this road once already. I made my way down the hall, checking each room as I went while Connie kept the hallway and our backs clear. It was slow going with office furniture and equipment laying everywhere. Whoever had done this had thoroughly trashed my doctor's office.

It took nearly ten minutes of careful checking to ensure that the clinic was clear and we were alone. As soon as we were sure of that Connie made a beeline to her drug safe. I imagined it had began it's life as a gun safe and been modified for medical use by the look of it. Set into the wall and anchored in concrete, the robbers had not been able to get inside the massive thing.

"Well, there's that, anyway," she sighed, leaning against the safe. "Damn what a mess," she added, looking around despondently.

"I'd guess that's why the place is trashed," I told her, holstering my pistol. "They couldn't get what they were after and decided to tear the office up instead."

"Bastards," Connie muttered. "Look at my records!" she almost wailed. "This will take days to straighten out!" I sympathized with her but it was time to call the police in on this. I tried an office phone and was surprised to get a dial tone. I called the police direct instead of 911.

"Police," a voice dulled by exhaustion answered after maybe seven rings.

"This is Shelton Drake," I said. "I'm at Doctor Kane's office on Temple and she's had a break-in. Can you send an officer?" I wasn't expecting to get anyone to be honest and I wasn't disappointed.

"Inventory what's missing and we'll generate a report from here for the insurance," the dispatcher said tonelessly. "I'm sorry, sir, but with everything that's happening that's about all we can do."

"I understand," I replied politely. "I assumed as much to be honest but decided we needed to call in to make sure."

"Thank you for understanding," the dispatcher said, her voice softening a bit. "Please be careful. Now that you're in the office they may return, especially if they think you have access to drugs."

"We'll watch ourselves," I promised and hung up. I looked at Connie who was still languishing over her medical records.

"No dice on the cops," I said evenly. "And the dispatcher warned that whoever did it might come back since they couldn't get the drugs. If they think someone's here who has access they might try again."

"I hope they do," Connie muttered dangerously. She was seriously pissed off and I couldn't blame her.

"Are your records backed up on disk?" I asked and she shook her head.

"No," she sighed. "I was going to transition into a new computer system later this year. Already had the set-up for it, just hadn't had the time. It's a lot of work to get all that turned over into computer records."

"If things straighten out I'll help you," I promised and she smiled at that.

"My very own computer nerd," she said softly and I laughed.

"I need to do something about that door and window I guess," I sighed. "Look, I don't want to leave you here alone but I'll need to go and get some plywood to close that up," I indicated the broken window and door. "I suppose we might get lucky and get them replaced but I wouldn't hold my breath."

"I was thinking the same thing," she admitted. "Give me a few minutes to see what's missing, if anything," she looked at her watch. "We won't be able to get into a hardware store before eight anyway," she added.

"I'll start cleaning up the glass," I nodded and she smiled again.

"I really appreciate that," she told me.

"Hey, it's what I live for."

*****

I gotta be honest, I hadn't expected any of Connie's staff to come in to work. I don't say that in any kind of bad or judgmental way, I just didn't expect it with everything like it was. It was dangerous just to be out, let along to be inside a doctor's office.

I also didn't think any of her patients would show up, either.

Wrong on both counts Drake.

Nettie Halliburton walked into the office at seven forty-five sharp just as I finished sweeping the last of the broken glass out of the waiting room. Nettie was a formidable looking woman. She wasn't quite as tall as Connie, but then Connie was maybe a millimeter under six feet. Halliburton was five-nine at a minimum and roughly as wide. Sorry, that's unfair.

It wasn't that she was fat. She wasn't. She was just. . .solid. Farm girl I guess. Tall, broad shouldered and just. . .solid. Best word I can come up with that's not going to sound ugly. She was probably in her late forties to early fifties.

"Who the hell are you?" she demanded as she walked through the broken door.

Very direct person, Nettie Halliburton. I may not have mentioned that at first.

"He's my boyfriend," Connie's voice drifted through the receptionist's window and once more I was the tallest man in town. I was her *boyfriend!* Hear that? Ha! I was about to smirk in typical male satisfaction when I realized that Nettie was still giving me the evil eye.

"So you got a name, boyfriend?" she asked just short of challenging.

"Ah, yes ma'am," I nodded, any thoughts about smirking gone. Did I mention how formidable Nettie was?

"And?" an eyebrow shot up in impatience.

"Uh, Drake," I replied. "Shelton Drake."

"I've seen you here before," her eyes narrowed at me and I nodded.

"Yes ma'am, you have," I agreed. "I was here last Monday."

"And now you're the boyfriend?" she snorted slightly.

"It's complicated," I tried, shrugging.

"Nettie, enough," Connie's voice came out of the office again. "I appreciate it but I can take care of myself. And he can take care of me, too," she added and the smirk threatened to blossom on my face again. I stuffed it back down, not wanting to get on Nettie's bad side. Or maybe worse side. I hadn't actually seen a good side yet.

"What the hell happened here, anyway?" she demanded through the window, ignoring me completely now. "What a mess."

"Someone broke in," Connie told her. "Probably after the drugs and when they couldn't get them they tore the place apart."

"Bastards," Nettie snarled. She looked back at me.

"You gonna stand there all day or fix that door?" Very formidable woman, Nettie.

*****

After Nettie Halliburton's 'suggestion' I decided that it was time to get started. Connie needed to stay and now that she wasn't alone I could spare the time to run to the nearest place and get a couple sheets of plywood.

"Need anything else?" I asked, making a short list of things I needed to at least close her office up and seal out the weather. Nothing I could do would keep her from being broken into again.

"A Coke would be nice," she admitted. "I don't usually drink soda regularly but I think I could use the sugar and caffeine today. Get me the one with sugar and not corn syrup. The Mexican Coke."

"You know that statement could result in a DEA investigation." That was what everyone called the 'export' soda, but I couldn't resist.

"Go!" she laughed, making a shooing motion. I looked at Nettie.

"Can I get you anything, ma'am?" I asked. Politely. Have I mentioned how formidable Nettie is?

"If you can find me about six storage tubs that would be great," she surprised me. "I need something to put the records in while we're sorting them," she added.

"Storage it is," I nodded. "Back soon!" I called and headed out. As I was leaving a woman with two kids was getting out of a car in the parking lot.

"Is the doctor seeing patients?" the woman asked, looking at the damaged front.

"I think so, but I'm not positive," I admitted. "The receptionist is inside," I pointed. The woman nodded and pulled her children to her, heading inside. I climbed into Big Baby and was soon weaving through traffic again.

*****

So. Plywood. Usually not a problem, right? That Monday was not a usual day. I tried three places including Lowes before I found two, that is *two* sheets of three-quarters plywood at a local hardware store. By two I mean *last* two. Probably in the whole town. I managed to get two more sheets of one inch plywood which for some reason was not as popular. There were *four* sheets of that left.

Taking my plunder I weaved and bobbed my way through the traffic once more to Connie's office. I pulled into a steadily filling parking lot. I had moved two chairs into the front before I left so I'd have room to work and miraculously no one had moved or run over them. Sometimes you get lucky. I backed into the spot and got out.

I delivered Connie's Coke and Nettie's storage tubs, noting that there were several people in the waiting room now. I looked at Nettie.

"We're the only ones here," she told me quietly.

"Anything I can do to help?" I asked.

"You can fix the window," she snorted. Got it. Boyfriend not needed. Message received. I went.

I have no idea why I had my tool box in the truck other than I had placed some things inside when all this had started. By sheer luck I had my battery powered drill and saw combo. Every once in a while you get lucky. I had probably had a reason for putting the box in there when I did it, and then had promptly forgotten it. Regardless, I had it with me, thank goodness.

I used the two chairs that had reserved my parking place as sawhorses and pulled the first sheet of wood out. Measuring the window first, I cut one of the one-inch board to fit and covered what was left of the window with it, using wood screws to hold it in place. I used a lot of them, hoping that would slow down another intruder. Might not make any difference, but the longer it took me to do this, the less time I had to spend around Nettie Halliburton. Have I mentioned how formidable Nettie is?

The door was a bit more trouble and it took me a while to work things out. I cut one of three-quarters boards to fit it and then drilled several holes around the edge. I then placed the plywood against the frame and drilled through those holes into the door. That took a while and I had to change the battery about half-way through it. Once finished I used some self tapping metal screws to attach the plywood to the frame. They would hold up longer than the door frame I was pretty sure. I remember looking at it and wishing I had gotten some paint. It didn't matter in the long run but. . .it felt incredibly right to be doing something like this for my lovely doctor. Like I was her hero. I know that sounds corny and I don't mean it that way, but it was like, she needed something done and I could do it, know what I mean? I wanted to make it look as good as possible.

Every man enjoys being able to do that. Be useful to the woman he loves. Any man who says he doesn't is either a liar or he's not really in love with the woman in question. I realize that's just my opinion but I'm convinced I'm right.

Anyway.

Finished with that I secured all my tools and locked Baby up to go inside. There was still the patient records door, but I needed to have a look at that. I didn't have a frame to work with there. I caught Connie coming out of an exam room as I stepped inside the hallway.

"Hey," she smiled and gave me a brief kiss. "How's it going?"

"Window and door are fixed," I told her. "How about you?"

"Thanks," she smiled. "It's crazy. No one but me and Nettie here. No nurse at all so I'm doing everything."

"You having Nettie call your other patients or are you going to try and see them?" I asked.

"I don't know," she admitted. "I. . .I want to be here for them," she said and I could tell it was pulling at her.

"If you want to be here, I'll do my best to get you here," I promised. "Do whatever you want and I'll be right here beside you." That statement earned me the lion-killer smile again. You remember the one? I hugged her briefly as she started to go into another room.

"I'll see if I can help Dragon Lady," I whispered and she giggled softly.

"She's a sweetheart, really," Connie whispered back, giving me one last peck on the cheek before ducking into the next patient room.

I walked back up to the reception area.

"Any way I can help?" I asked again.

"Can you take vitals?" Nettie asked in a huff. Sweetheart. Right.

"Yes, I can," I replied and got to see Nettie looked flummoxed. Which in turn made all the time and money spent on classes so worth it.

"What?"

"Yes, I can take vitals," I repeated, and this time I allowed my inner smirk to be free. Take that!

"Well, you may not be completely useless after all," she recovered quickly. The bitch. She thrust a stethoscope at me.

"Take this and get started," she ordered. "If the red tab is out, then there's a patient waiting for you to take vitals. While you're doing that try and get a general sense of what the problem is and write that down for Connie. Once you come out, put the red tab in, pull the green one out, and leave the chart in the receptacle on the door. Got it?"

"I'm sure I can do at least half that," I nodded and she snorted.

"That's about what I've got figured."

And so that's how I became a physician's assistant as the zombie apocalypse was breaking out across the world.

CHAPTER TEN

It was nearly six o'clock by the time we'd seen the last patient. There had been down time between patients at time, but never more than maybe fifteen minutes. During that time I had managed to repair the shattered records room door using the old door and some three-quarters plywood sheeting. It looked like crap but it would at least allow them to close and lock the door. I made a quick run to the nearest store that I could find a hasp and padlock for the door and put it on there to give them some security. It wouldn't do anything but keep honest people honest, but Connie could truthfully say that her records had been secured behind a locked door.

I'd like to tell you that Nettie Halliburton warmed up to me as the day went along but. . .I'd be lying. About the best I managed was the 'you're not useless' tag. I didn't know if it was a problem with me personally, which I saw no way it could be, or if she was just very protective of Connie. I didn't have a problem with

239

protective since I felt the same way, but. . .I have to admit that her attitude was really wearing on me by the end of the day.

I have no idea how many times I checked blood pressure, temperature, weight, all that crap that gets done before you actually get to see the doctor. It's not a challenge, nor is it difficult, but it is boring as hell after you get the rhythm down. Still, Connie was doing everything else alone so whatever I could do to make it easier on her I was going to do it.

I almost washed the skin off my hands in the process. I wore gloves each time but. . .did I mention how I was becoming a germaphobe? Now I was actually having to *touch* people. *Sick* people. It literally made my skin crawl. I was sneezed on at least three times while taking vitals. Once by a kid that I am certain did it on purpose, the little shit. It's very easy when people start doing that kind of thing, or letting their kids do it, to start hoping someone actually *does* get eaten by zombies. I mean very easy.

In between doing that and fixing the door I also managed to clean up the rest of the mess left behind by the break in and take out the trash. I swept the hallway out and cleaned the exam rooms as they were emptied at the end of the day. It sounds like a lot but really it wasn't. It kept me busy but that was about all.

As the final patient left for the day I noticed a car sitting in the parking lot with three men inside. I pretended to sweep the front walk while I kept an eye on them. I couldn't see out from the office thanks to the board replacing the window. This was trouble. I knew it was and started wondering what to do about it.

I called the police again and got a different dispatcher. This one was a man and wasn't quite as polite as the woman earlier in the day had been. I relayed to him the fact that the office had been burglarized and that there were three men sitting outside the office in a parked car at that very moment, watching the place.

"What do you want me to do about it?" the asshole had demanded.

"Well, I thought you might want to send someone up here to check them out, since this office had already been burglarized and we're getting ready to close up. It's possible they will attack the women who work here in an attempt to get at the drugs stored here."

"If that happens call back. We'll deal with it then," the jackass snarled and then hung up. I cursed him and most of three generations of his family as I put my phone up, wishing I could see outside. I found Connie making notes about the last of her patients in her small office.

"We may have a problem," I told her.

"Well, today has gone so well we had to expect a little trouble," she shot back. Took me a second to get that she was joking.

"There's a car with three guys in it outside, just watching the place," I told her. "I called the police and the dispatcher basically told me to go screw myself. Call back if they attacked. Of course if I do call back it'll be for the M.E. again," I said evenly.

"What do we do?" she asked.

"Can we go out the back?" I asked. There was a back door, but I hadn't opened it or checked it out.

"We can, but there's no room back there for a car, let alone that monster you drive," Connie told me.

"I can move around the end of the building so we can get in that way," I said. "Once we're in, we can pull around front and block the door from their view while Nettie gets to her car and leaves. If they get out we can shoot them," I shrugged.

"I'd prefer not to have to shoot anyone," Connie frowned.

"So would I, but I'm not about to let anything happen to you," I said plainly. "Not going to happen." She smiled softly at that but nodded her acceptance.

"I know the Chief of Police," Connie said. "Let me call him and see if he can get someone up here. It might be that they aren't up to anything."

"Might be I'm a movie star," I snorted. "I'll be in the waiting room," I told her as she picked up the phone.

The phones had been working today without any problem. Maybe the problem Saturday had just been jammed circuits, I didn't know. I'd been busy today so I'd seen no news to amount to anything, just snatched on the waiting room television set as I was in and out.

I got to the waiting room and locked the door, something I should have done earlier. With the board in place we couldn't see out and that made us vulnerable. I didn't like that but it was what it was. For the moment we were stuck with it.

I turned the television to a news channel and turned the volume up a bit. I'd already cleaned the waiting room and wiped the seats and fixtures down with Lysol. Germaphobe, remember?

"What are you doing?" Nettie demanded from behind her receptionist glass.

"This is a television," I pointed to the screen, tired of her shit. "If you watch this while it's tuned to a news channel, you might find shit out. I'm trying to find shit out." With that I placed Nettie on Ignore and turned back to the screen. She mumbled something behind me but. . .Ignore.

Things had not improved during the day and were expected to get worse with nightfall. I checked my watch. It was about twenty minutes til seven. Late to still be out and about but Connie was having to do her job and then the work normally done by her nurses.

Every state except Alaska had called out their National Guard to help quell disturbances in their major cities. I guess Alaska didn't have as many idiots as the rest of us. Or maybe it was just too cold for protests there, I didn't know.

Dumbo hadn't been on television anymore and there had been only the standard messages from the rest of the stooges in Washington. You know the ones. No reason to panic. Situation under control. All precautions taken. Irresponsible people simply adding to the problem. That last part was true but then it always was. Basically nothing had changed since Saturday from the government prospective. The news was still running the 'precautions' that the Surgeon General had given, and the more conservative shows were interviewing 'noted physicians' who all said the same thing Connie had; bullshit. They made the same arguments she had. Nothing special in these warnings. They were literally the same good health advice that all doctors gave their patients.

The looting, shooting and rioting had eased off during the day but as night was approaching the activity was picking back up. Police had their hands full to say the least. Store owners were fighting back, shooting rioters who tried to steal or burn their stores. Police in at least one city had tried to arrest a store owner while thieves were actually hauling shit out of his store, all caught on tape by a news crew. The surprise was when other store owners on the block had come to his rescue and beat the shit out of the two cops and then shot maybe five or six more looters before the rest had run off.

More cops had shown up after a frantic call by the two idiot cops, resulting in a standoff between the store owners and the cops. A news crew managed to get by the cops and interview the store owners live as they stood their ground. Public opinion was firmly on the side of the store owners according to e-mails and tweets and Facebook posts, making me wonder who in the hell had time to be posting on Facebook and Twitter at a time like this.

The cops finally backed down. You couldn't hear what was being said but I'm sure from the finger pointing and grandstanding the the cops were giving the 'we'll be back speech'. None of the store owners looked intimidated. Good for them. I heard Connie calling and turned away from the vigilante justice to see what she'd found out.

"There should be a car here in a few minutes," Connie told me. "The Chief is a patient," she shrugged. "He asked for the dispatcher's name but I didn't have it. Sorry."

"Better that way, probably," I shrugged.

"He said to tell you 'nice job' by the way," Connie added. "And not to worry about it, especially now."

"Especially now that the zombie apocalypse is upon us or especially now that I'm your boyfriend?" I couldn't help asking, grinning widely.

"He didn't say," she shrugged. "Either way it's good news."

"True," I nodded. Before I could say anything else I saw a squad car pull up in the parking lot. I looked at Connie and Nettie.

"Get your things, we're out of here while they're on the scene."

"I still have work to do," Connie protested.

"Dark soon," I shook my head. "If you want we can take it with us but we will be home behind the fence before the sun goes down." She looked as if she might argue but I stood my ground. I knew I was right and she did too.

"He's right," Nettie said abruptly, which almost caused me to lose my tough guy composure. "Let him get you out of here and safe." She glared at me as if warning me but I just snorted.

"You too, then," Connie ordered. "Will you help me?" she asked me.

"Of course I will," I manged to both look and sound offended. We hurried to her office and loaded all the files she still had to update into one of the storage tubs which I immediately took and loaded in the back of the Blazer. Nettie was already out the door and to her car. She looked back once more and actually waved. For the first time she looked sad, maybe even a little pensive.

"I swear I'll take care of her," I called gently, just loud enough she could hear me. "It'll be over my dead body and empty gun." Nettie gave me a long look and then nodded once before getting into her car and leaving. I glanced over to where one cop was talking to the driver while another was covering the car with a shotgun. I could hear the cop getting a little louder than a simple, routine call should have warranted.

Connie came out behind me with an honest to God Doctor's bag in her hand.

"I didn't know they still made those," I almost goggled. "Cool!" She shook her head as she laughed and handed me the bag which I loaded into the back. I was still trying to keep at least one eye on the cops.

"Anything?" she asked.

"No idea," I admitted. "Are you ready?" I asked. I wanted to take advantage of the cops being on the scene to get Connie out of there.

"Yes," she nodded and turned to lock the door. It wouldn't probably keep anyone out, but it was better than nothing. We had strengthened the interior doors and the records were locked in a closet that I had added a padlock and hasp to. Wasn't much but better than nothing.

I helped Connie into the passenger seat and then crawled into the driver's seat, my attention still on the car. The cop with the shotgun had moved closer and was giving the car his undivided attention. I took that as a sign of escalation. I wanted to stay and make sure they made it okay, but not as much as I wanted Connie safe. Connie's safety won out and I pulled away from the building. I noted that the guy in the passenger seat was giving us the eye. I knew right then I'd likely have trouble with that guy. There was no hiding Big Baby so it wasn't like he couldn't find me again.

'Well, you just come and look, buddy', I thought to myself, smirking just a little at him. *'I got something for you.'*

"Stop trying to stare them down," Connie said, interrupting my man-moment. I turned to look at her.

"How are you doing that?" I demanded.

"Doing what?" she asked, fighting off a yawn.

"It's like you're reading your mind," I complained.

"No, I'm not. You're a man, that's all. Pretty easy to figure out what you're thinking."

I was absolutely sure there was an insult in there somewhere but. . .well, I was driving, that's all. I had to concentrate on my driving. Traffic and all. You know.

In the back of my mind though I just knew we'd see those three again. I needed to be ready for that when it came.

Believe it or not, Jacks was open. I looked hopefully at Connie and she sighed and nodded so I whipped into the parking lot. Five minutes later we were back on the road with three, that's *three* juicy, delicious Double Big Jack cheeseburgers and two orders of fries. Oh and Connie got some kind of salad with chicken or whatever.

I hummed all the way home.

*****

Once we were home I made sure the gate was shut hard. I hadn't let the chickens out today so I went and gave them plenty of food and freshened their water before going inside. I stopped in the garage to put the batteries to my power tools on the charger. Might need them again.

Once inside I opened a Dr. Pepper and settled in front of the television to watch the world implode or be over-run with zombies, whichever came first. From the look of things the zombies weren't going to get the chance to destroy the world because the other zombies were doing it first.

You know there should be some kind of law against stupid. I have no idea how you could enforce it but there should be something to protect the rest of us. Right?

I gobbled down my first burger with CNN, and then turned to Fox. The news was pretty much the same with only a few details missing. I didn't bother with anything else. I did hit the 'net and check for new stories though. There was a lot going on and I realized that Harold Falter had been right on the money.

Video from New York was on the internet now showing the same kind of behavior and attacks that the amateur video from Spain had shown us. There were official denials of course, and charges of a hoax, but you could tell the responses were canned. The story was probably right on.

More from two other places, Boston and a small town near Baltimore. I can't remember the name of the place. I suppose history recorded it somewhere. I mean assuming history didn't get eaten by zombies. I just can't remember the name or I'd record it here.

Anyway, the situation was getting out of hand and doing so in a hurry. I started on my second burger, leaning back to watch the web videos and read the comments. I hate to admit it but. . .I read the comments just to see what kind of stupid shit some people were posting. You know the ones, I know you do. You laugh at them too. Or did.

Anyway that's what I was doing when Connie came into the living room fresh from the shower and sat down with me, opening her chicken salad. . .chicken with salad. . .no, salad with chicken? Opening her food and a bottle of water.

"Those things will kill you," she warned me, looking at my burger.

"Not going to get the chance, probably," I shrugged. "And to be honest, I used to eat there maybe once, twice a month. Knowing I might be cut off any day though has forced me to take drastic action and stock up now for the dry times." I said all this with a completely straight face. Mostly because I meant it.

Connie looked at me for maybe five full seconds and then burst into laughter. I shrugged and took another bite.

"So what's happening," she asked, nodding her head toward the screen.

"New York, Boston, and a place outside Baltimore," I told her, turning the screen where she could see better. "Those are the only places in the states with what they're calling 'confirmed cases'. As you can see from the video, a 'confirmed case' is one that involves running through the streets in disarray and attacking anyone that gets within reach."

It was true, too. The brief video from New York was almost a carbon copy of the original video that had started me on this odyssey.

"So do we think it's going to spread, or will we by some miracle be spared?" Connie asked, forking at her salad.

"I honestly don't know," I admitted. "What I'm worried about is that this," I pointed at the screen, "is just what we know about. For every story that's making the news there could be another, or ten or whatever, that isn't in the public view yet. No way to know what's going on elsewhere unless we see it here."

"True," she nodded. "I think tomorrow is it, Drake," she said after a minute. "I want to go into the office tomorrow and see whoever shows up. After that I'll take it day by day until this settles down some. Do you think we'll have trouble with those guys who were in the parking lot?"

"Probably," I admitted. "I hope not, and maybe they were doing something that the cops could bust them for and put them away. But we can't count on that so we need to be cautious. Don't take it for granted that we'll be safe, from them or anyone else. You can bet they aren't the only ones who might think that a doctor's office is a good target."

"I don't even keep anything like they'd want," Connie sighed. "I don't keep painkillers or other narcotics in my office. Just things like flu vaccine, tetanus shots, insulin, vitamins and stuff like that. There's not a single thing in that drug safe that's worth a dime on the streets."

"Stupid people do stupid things every day," I shrugged. "They aren't smart enough maybe to know that. I don't really have an answer for you on that score, Connie."

We ate in silence for several minutes after that, each thinking our own thoughts I guess. It was a comfortable silence, looking back. It still surprises me how easily we slipped into a comfortable role with each other. It makes me wish I had asked her out earlier. You know, before the world ended. How much did we miss because I was too scared to suck it up and approach her?

Anyway, it was suddenly almost ten. I had put my third and possibly last cheeseburger in the refrigerator to save for another time. Like, tomorrow. I walked into the bedroom, undressed and climbed into the shower. By the time I was finished I was feeling the stress of the day I admit it. The work hadn't been all that hard but the strain of how things were was starting to tell. I was tired and knew that we had to do it all again tomorrow. I was under no illusion that Connie's staff would show up tomorrow either. Maybe, but not likely.

I walked into the bedroom to find myself in a candlelit scene of beautiful woman and soft scents. Connie was lying on her side across the foot of my, uh our, king size bed, head propped on her hand, waiting for me.

"Evening, stranger," she purred seductively. "What'cha doin'?"

"Whatever you want," I admitted, suddenly no longer tired.

Nope. Not tired at all.

CHAPTER ELEVEN

The next day sucked. That's putting it mildly. We made the trip into town hoping to find that things had calmed down but it was not to be. If anything conditions were worse than before. None of the accidents had yet been cleared and there were several more to add to it now. Traffic could still move, but it was limited to say the least.

We still managed to make it into the office where I was relieved to see that the boards were still up and in place. I noticed that the car from the day before was still where it had been and hoped that meant that the three guys who had been inside were now resting peacefully in jail. That would simplify things greatly.

By eight fifteen Nettie was still not in the office and no patients were waiting. I looked over the appointment calender and noted that several people had called in to cancel or postpone their appointments. Gotta say I was surprised that anyone would think to do that under the circumstances. Gave me a better appreciation of why Connie wanted to make sure her patients were cared for. At least some of them were good enough to call and let her know they weren't going to be in to see her right here at the end of the world.

By nine we were still alone and Connie started going through her office selecting things she wanted to carry home with us.

"I'm not coming back until this is over unless I have to," she told me as we packed one of the storage tubs I had gotten the day before with her things. "It's not. . .it's too dangerous and it's not worth it anymore." She sounded tired and dejected. On impulse I took her in my arms and hugged her tight, rubbing her back.

"Don't think like that," I told her gently. "You came to make sure your patients were taken care of and that's worth it. You've done all you can and that's always going to be all you can do." I held her for another minute and then she pushed away far enough to look up at me.

"Why didn't you ask me out sooner?" she asked.

"Scared," I shrugged. It has always amazed me how much her thoughts seem to roll right with mine.

"Of what?"

"Rejection of course," I told her easily. "You're smart, beautiful, funny, successful. I mean what man isn't intimidated by that."

"It's not like I'm the best looking woman in town," she snorted.

"I beg to differ," I shrugged again. "You are all that and more and I was just wondering the same thing last night. How much had we missed together because I'm basically a coward at heart."

"Drake, you may be a lot of things but you're certainly not a coward," Connie snorted. "No coward would have done what you did Saturday night for two teenagers he never met before."

"That was easy," I scoffed. "All that took was some training and a complete lack of good judgment. We're talking about something way more serious than that." She laughed at that and wiped a tear away.

"Enough of this," I told her firmly. "You've done all you can do. It's time to look

N.C. REED

after yourself. What else do I need to load
up?" She nodded and started again packing
things she wanted to save.

As I made each trip to the vehicle I
made sure to case the parking lot and the
area around us. I didn't have any kind of
bad feeling, I was just being cautious. The
last few days had shown that we needed
caution.

It took maybe another hour for Connie
to go through everything and get what she
wanted or needed. By the time she was
finished I had packed the Blazer pretty tight
but she had everything she wanted. She
locked the now wooden door with a sigh. I
had placed a sign on the door and the
window with a brief message that the office
was closed due to the break-in and the
current crisis and would re-open as soon as
the situation allowed. That was probably a
bit optimistic, I knew even then, but. . .you
know.

"I worked so hard to get this far," she
told me sadly. "All that for nothing, now, it
looks like."

"Not for nothing," I insisted. "You've helped a great many people in your work. And this may not be so bad as you think," I reminded her. "We might be back here in a week putting all this stuff back. Let's not borrow trouble, okay?" She smiled and nodded, hugging be briefly.

"I'm lucky to have you," she said suddenly, and I managed to nod.

"You certainly are," I smiled and winked. "Now, get in the car, Doctor Hottie." She giggled at that and I helped her climb aboard. She had taken most everything that meant anything to her and emptied her drug safe into a cooler.

I drove to Co-op again to fuel up. There was a slight line this time but not much and I soon had Big Baby topped off and ready for action. Two stations I had passed already had signs out that said they were out of gas, and I wondered how much longer there would be fuel anywhere in town. Things were growing worse by the hour and from the look of it the non-infected people were doing far more damage so far than the infected. It was time to head home.

"Why don't we drive through town one last time," I said on a whim. No idea why I said it. There was no reason to. We had everything we could think of. It was just a notion that hit me.

"Okay," Connie shrugged. "Might as well." I could tell she was really down in the dumps. I tried to think of something to cheer her up as I drove.

Town was a real mess to say the least. We stayed on the main drags, so to speak, just looking at the various stores and businesses. There were signs of vandalism and destruction on nearly every block. We saw a few places still open, including one little independent type grocery that was being guarded by a man on the roof. He stood over the entrance way holding a pump shotgun, a grim look on his face. The small store had two semi-trailers backed up to the rear, surrounded by a chain link fence. It struck me suddenly that if they had access to a dependable water supply, that was a good place to hole up. I said as much to Connie and she studied the place.

"Might be," she agreed with a nod after her inspection. "I wonder if that fence was already up before all this started or if he managed to get it in place afterward," she mused. "I can't remember one way or another," she admitted.

"I'm pretty sure it was already there," I told her, trying to keep the conversation going to take her mind off her practice. "It think that used to be something else and the fence basically came with the building. Coming in handy now."

"Sure is," she nodded. "How about that convenience store?" she pointed to a quick stop style C-Store. "Looks like they've got shutters similar to yours. Wonder if they can access the roof from inside?"

And so it went as we rolled through town for what might be the last time. We didn't know at the time, one way of the other, you know? We had spent a madcap week in preparation for something we hoped wouldn't happen and in the process had missed a lot of what was happening day to day in town. We could see several places that looked as if their owners were going to make that were they stood or fell if the worst came to pass. Other places looked as if they'd been completely abandoned.

We saw no looting or violence or other trouble during out drive, but the signs were everywhere. We passed at least three places that I can remember where a building had been damaged or destroyed by fire. That made me wonder if the fire department was still active. It also gave me an inspiration that I wished I had gotten earlier. I wheeled around in the middle of the street and headed for the Tractor Supply.

"Drake, what's wrong?" Connie demanded.

"I got an idea, I just hope I'm not too late," I told her. "I just thought of something that will help with our water problem!"

"What is it?"

"Stock tanks!" I almost crowed. I don't know why I hadn't thought of it before and I don't know why thinking about the fire department made me think of it then, but a stock tank, or two, placed in the back yard and filled with water could give us another four, maybe five hundred gallons of potable water.

"You mean like for a farm?" she asked and I nodded.

"Is that safe to drink?"

"I don't see why not, and anyway we'll filter it if we have to drink it," I replied as I turned into the parking lot. I immediately saw two of the desired products sitting behind the fence. The store was still open, though it looked as if they were closing soon as the employees were moving stuff inside. I jumped out of the Blazer and headed inside, Connie right behind me.

Ten minutes later I had purchased three two-hundred gallon tanks at the half-off, end-of-the-world sale price. The manager gave me a key to the lock on the gate which surprised me.

"You could have just waited and stole them," he shrugged. "Since you didn't, I'd say you're pretty honest. Just leave the key inside the fence, under that trough, there will be fine," he pointed out a watering trough. I thanked him and grabbed Connie by the hand, heading back to the Blazer.

"What are you doing?" she demanded as we got in.

"I need to go get my trailer to haul these things," I told her. "If I hurry I might get back in time to get some help loading them." We literally raced home, running several stop signs along the way. I pulled into the yard as soon as the gate opened and drove straight around back to where my flat-bottomed trailer set. I hadn't used it in a while, but thankfully the tires were still up. I hurriedly hooked up, Connie not even getting out of the Blazer. In five minutes we were on our way back to town.

I ran the same stop signs in reverse getting back and believe it or not made it with five minutes to spare. The manager just shook his head as he and another employee motioned for me to pull up alongside the gate. Together we loaded all three tanks on my sixteen-foot trailer and lashed them down. I handed the key back to the man, thanking them.

They were heading to their own cars as we pulled out of the parking lot headed home once more. It was a slower trip this time as I didn't want to risk losing one of the tanks.

"I think I'll leave them on the trailer, maybe," I said as we neared the house. "If we need to move the tanks, it would be impossible to do without emptying the water first. Once we lose the utility, we can't refill them."

"You won't need the trailer for something else?" Connie asked.

"I don't think so," I shrugged. "I mean, this is our bug-out location. We're set up here and don't really have a fall back. Do we?" I asked, looking at her.

"No," she sighed. "Not that I can think of, anyway. I'd always thought I'd have one some day, but it doesn't look like that's going to happen."

"Hey, you got one here!" I pointed out and she smiled at me.

Once we were home I pulled around back again and parked the trailer near the house. I grabbed the water hose and lashed the nozzle to the mouth of the first tank and turned the water on. It would take a while to fill all three so I didn't waste time.

Connie went inside and soon Ram was running all over the yard like he'd lost his mind, yapping at everything he could see and stopping every five feet to pee. He saw the chickens still in their coop and caught another gear, running so fast that he tripped over his own feet once getting to the enclosure where he spent at least two full minutes chasing the chickens up and down the little fence. I finally managed to corral him and get him back inside.

I released the chickens to roam the yard and get some exercise while I took my rifle and walked the fence. Seems a little extreme I guess, but things were getting ugly and I didn't want to be caught by surprise. It took me about twenty minutes to make that round and by the time I got back Connie had changed out of her Doctor Hottie uniform and had fixed us some lunch. I cleaned up and we took our sandwiches into the living room so that we could catch up on what was happening while we ate.

The wheels were coming off of society and we had tried to be ready for it. It was time to take advantage of all that preparation and try and survive whatever was coming down the pike.

Including friggin' zombies, man.

*****

In hindsight I should have expected it, but all I can say is that I wasn't really thinking about it. That changed with a phone call. Connie's cell started ringing, her ring tone from Phantom of the Opera.

"Hey, Music of the Night!" I enthused. Connie looked at me a bit funny as she accepted the call.

"Kane." So authoritative. I liked that.

"No, my office was burglarized two nights ago, approximately. I've closed it until further notice." All I could get was her side of the conversation, but I noted a frown on her beautiful features.

"Well, I'm not going to do that," I heard her say rather firmly. "No way. And I've already served my time working with DWB.

Yes, it does, I made sure of that." I was frowning now. What the hell was all this?

"That I'm willing to do so long as I can guarantee my own safety," she said after a minute. "Don't throw that crap at me, I'm not listening to it, from you or anyone else. Of course I'm willing to help and how dare you remind me of my oath!"

Uh-oh.

"Well you should remember that calling with threats and blackmail aren't the best way to get cooperation from anyone. As I said I'm willing to work in the local hospital, but that's all you get from me. There's absolutely no way I'm going into the city and that's final."

What? Oh *hell* no.

"I don't work for the hospital, Madeline. I have patients there sometimes and when I do I make rounds. I also work the ER about once every blue moon to fill in for others who are on vacation." Pause. "Well at this point I don't think that losing my hospital privileges is going to have that great an impact on my practice."

"Yes, I'm willing to do that so long as I can guarantee my own safety, as I said. Yes, that means I'll be armed." Pause. "I'm well aware of the hospital's policy and I don't care. If you want me to help out I'm glad to do so, but only under those conditions. I have no intention of putting myself at risk any more than I already have. I risked robbery at gun point to open my clinic and see my patients yesterday and today even with the front window and front door of my office destroyed, so please don't presume to lecture me about my responsibility as a doctor. I notice you aren't going into the city, now are you?" Longer pause.

"I didn't think so," the sarcasm in Connie's voice was clear. Pause. "I'll take the day shift," she said finally. "Then you can let some of the men work the late shift, Madeline. In case you haven't noticed things are not so great out at the moment and I'm not going to be traveling after dark, alone, just so some old fuddy you used to sleep around with can be comfortable on days." I clamped both hands over my mouth to keep from laughing out loud. My antics drew a sharp look from Connie but I was doing my best.

"Fine, I'll see you in the morning. I'll work seven to three, but know that it's on a day-to-day basis. If things continue to worsen then I'm out." Pause. "I'm sure you will, if you don't get eaten by zombies first." Pause. "I have no idea what they actually eat, but there's no reason I can't be hopeful."

At that point I had to get up and leave the room, hovering at the kitchen door so I could still hear but not burst out laughing and interrupt her call.

"Then I'll see you in the morning, Madeline. Oh, and I better not be short staffed either. No leaving me hanging on days to pad the night shift with extra help. I don't mind working but I'll be damned if I carry anyone else." Pause. "You know damn well I'll never see a penny from this, Madeline, either from you or the patients, so that's an empty threat. Now do you want me to work or not? Those are my terms and they are non-negotiable." Pause.

"Then as I said, I'll see you in the morning." With that she cut the phone off and I thought she was going to hurl it against the wall but she thought better of it and threw a pillow instead.

"Be hard to replace this thing right now," she looked at me. "I'm sure you've figured out by now that they want me to come work at the hospital."

"I got that drift, yeah," I nodded, easing back into the living room.

"Wrinkled old bitch," she muttered. "I hate that witch, I really do. She's tried her best to make my life miserable since I got here."

"Probably jealous," I shrugged. "What can I do to help?" I asked, and was rewarded once more with the lion-killer smile.

"Thanks, Drake," she leaned against me and kissed me lightly. "I'm sorry."

"About what? Being mad? Sounded like she was trying to blackmail you into going into the city."

"That's exactly what she was doing," Connie's frown returned. "She tried threatening me with the 'public service' clause in my loan contracts, but I reminded her that I already fulfilled mine when I was with Doctors Without Borders. Then she tried to threaten me by withdrawing my hospital privileges. An empty threat considering. I'm not going into the city and that's final. I will work locally so long as it's reasonably safe," she added. "Though I don't know how long that will be."

"Well, so long as you're armed, you can keep yourself safe. And I'll be close by," I added.

"You can't just hang around the hospital all day," Connie shook her head.

"Can if I want," I shot back with a mock pout that made her laugh.

"Anyway, there 'll be something I can do in town I'm sure," I waved away the protest. "If nothing else I'll volunteer at the hospital. I can help do something. And if things get too hot then we can load up and scoot."

"All right," she nodded. "Honestly I don't mind helping at the hospital, it's just that her attitude is so. . .so. . .*shitty*!" I looked at her for maybe three seconds before busting out laughing. She glared at me for a few seconds but soon enough was laughing along with me.

"All right," I said finally. "We're still free for the rest of the day, so let's get back to watching things unfold and try to get as much information as we can. Might help tomorrow," I pointed out.

"It might at that," she agreed. "And I am hungry. Arguing with that bitch always makes me like that." She looked at me again suddenly.

"You recognized my ring tone," she said it as a statement rather than a question.

"I did," I nodded, smiling. "Love the Phantom of the Opera."

"It's one of my favorite things," she said with a soft smile.

"Have you ever seen the live performance from Prince Albert Music Hall?" I asked. "I think it was the twenty-fifth anniversary," I added.

"No," she shook her head.

"Then you, my dear darling Doctor Hottie are in for a treat, because I happen to have a copy," I told her, smiling. "Let's fix us a bite and I'll put the DVD in!"

"I'm in," she nodded at once.

And that was how we spent our afternoon.

*****

I was up, as usual, long before daylight. I eased out, careful not to wake Connie knowing she would be likely to have a hectic day ahead, and went to the living room, turning on the television. It was apparent almost immediately that the situation was growing still worse.

One of the things that caught my eye was that the 'outbreaks' in the major cities were being openly acknowledged by officials now. There was still nothing from Dumb-asses of Columbia, but state and local officials in several areas were now on the record as having 'officially' recognized the 'seriousness of the situation concerning this disturbing phenomenon'.

Translation; shit has done got real and we don't know what to do.

There were now videos of apparent zombie attacks all over and even a few live streams from various local news agencies that maintained 'city cams'. DOT cameras on highways were also recording violence and 'uprisings' as some termed it. I shook my head at that. Even now, with clear evidence of what was happening, so many were still trying to rationalize what was happening, explain it away as some kind of civil disturbance.

They would either learn to accept and adapt, or. . .well, they'd probably be eaten. One or the other. I shrugged it away. At this point I was concentrating on myself and Connie and not much else.

I took my laptop to the kitchen and booted it up while I started some breakfast. I cruised through news sites and some medical web pages as well, looking for anything that might be helpful down the road. To be honest there wasn't much available other than panicky hyperbole at that point.

By the time I had breakfast ready my lovely doctor came stumbling into the kitchen in a tank top and some remarkably short shorts. She honestly had no concept of how hot she truly was. Seriously.

"Not really a morning person are you, sweetheart?" I asked with a smile, holding a cup of coffee under her nose as she sat down.

"Oh, thank you," her eyes opened a bit wider and she accepted the cup gratefully. "And no, not so much. You'd think I would get used to it after a while, but. . .I guess I worked too many nights when I was in residency."

"No problem," I assured her as I slid a plate in front of her with pancakes and bacon.

"You really will make someone a fine wife one day," she grinned as she dug into the meal I'd made her.

"I'm hoping so," I smiled as I sat down with my own plate. We ate in relative silence as I turned the laptop where we could both see the screen and we watched the news, such as it was, while we ate. It was honestly just repeats of the same tired things for the most part.

"When are they going to get a clue?" Connie muttered, shaking her head at one reporter's attempt to blame 'radicals' for the 'disturbances currently rocking the nation'.

"They don't want one," I shrugged. "As long as they don't say it, don't talk about it, it's not real to them in their ivory towers."

"It'll be real enough when someone takes a chunk out of their leg," she said flatly and I had to agree.

Honestly I kinda blame Hollywood for this one. Well, no, that's not fair either. I blame people who can't separate what Hollywood produces from what's real. Just like those idiots on the web earlier in the week giving 'advice' on *'how to deal with the 'undead menace'*, these reporters couldn't separate the truth from fiction. Since 'zombies' was a Hollywood construct, they couldn't possibly be real.

Newsflash; Holly-weird got the idea from *somewhere!* Zombies had been a part of almost every culture since before real written records. Was it real then? No idea. My point is that because they had 'seen' the movies, and maybe read the books, that meant that a real life zombie apocalypse couldn't be possible because it was a fantasy; science fiction.

Unfortunately they were about to get a wake-up call and it would be costly.

"We go now to Kelly Amberly who is on the scene in Overtown Square where there have been some minor incidents already this morning. Kelly?"

"Thank you Tom," the blonde said. You could tell she was scared. *"It's really not accurate to say there's been incidents already this morning because the incidents haven't really slowed overnight. It's just a continuation of what's been happening for the last two or three days. Behind me you can see Overtown Place which up until early this morning was actually a very nice three story mall of small specialty shops and cafes. Now it's mostly a burned husk, destroyed by fire sometime after it closed early last evening due to the disturbances in the area around us."*

"As the camera pans the area you can see that a few firefighters are still on the scene along with police as there appear to

still be several demonstrators in the area. We tried earlier to speak with some of the protesters to find out exactly what they're protesting this morning, but very few would even acknowledge us and none would speak on camera. They wouldn't give a reason for that, simply ignoring us altogether when we'd try to interview them. Officers we've spoken to in the last few minutes say that there is at least a temporary truce between the protesters and authorities while the fire and EMS services try to search for injured and ensure that the fire is completely out."

"Kelly is there any idea about how the fire started as yet?" Tom asked, to which I rolled my eyes. Who really gave a shit how the fire started at this point?

"The investigation is still in preliminary stages and authorities are reluctant to speculate about possible causes at this time, Tom. In fact the arson investigator we spoke to said that due to hot spots in the structure that the investigation wouldn't truly begin until sometime later today once the building was made as secure as possible."

"Now the interesting thing here is that the crowd that was here a few hours ago apparently ran from the fire in fear, at least that's what a few witnesses are saying off camera. None are willing to speak to us on camera at the moment because, to be honest, they're afraid the crowd will return and they're hiding. You can see as the camera scans the neighborhood around us that many homes are now boarding up windows with whatever materials they can find. Several of the people we spoke to said that the violence of the crowd was startling, putting the older residents in mind of the fire and police riots of the mid-seventies."

I hadn't been around for that, but everyone I'd ever spoken to had agreed that it had been a very rough time. I shuddered to think that this was worse, but. . .there was a reason those people were boarding up their homes. And a good reason they weren't talking to the news team. No one wanted to spend time in the loony bin with the end of the world on the horizon.

"Kelly, we're seeing some kind of disturbance among the people behind the

tape, there," Tom cut into my thinking. "Is there some kind of scuffle going on among the protesters?"

"I don't. . .wait, I can see now, Tom. It does appear that an altercation is taking place behind the police barrier. . .okay, officers on the scene are moving into the area. . .oh my . . . Tom, I don't know if you can see but there's a large gathering of people behind the protesters who are. . .George can you get that? who are apparently attacking someone. . .no it's more like several someones. . .Tom it appears that a brawl has broken out here in the area behind the protesters as police are moving in to try and secure the area, I can see two officers trying to subdue. . .George we may need to move back some. . .there's an officer down! Tom there's an officer down now as others are trying to move in and contain the situat- oh my God!"

We both stopped eating as the camera view bobbed and weaved a bit. You could still hear Amberly babbling as the camera man tried to put some distance between himself and the crowd while still getting at least some footage.

There was the sound of clamoring in the background and a good bit of thumping and bumping. After about three minutes the camera righted and it was obvious that the crew was at a much higher angle now.

"We're on top of the Channel 5 News van now, Tom," Amberly sounded shaky. *"We're safe here, I think, and you can get a better idea of what's happening in the crowd. George have you got the camera rolling?"* Muttered reply. *"Well you don't have to be rude about it!"* Amberly snapped. *"Anyway, Tom it's apparent that those who had fled the scene may have returned and started a brawl with peaceful protesters. I apologize for my outburst earlier but I could have sworn I saw. . .well, never mind about that now. As we. . .George, what is it? Why are. . .where are you going? Get your ass back here, we're on live!"*

We both leaned in to the screen as the situation went from bad to very bad for Amberly the snappy reporter person. George the rude camera man had obviously had enough and fled the scene as the camera was now aimed down at the street beside the van.

So that we could see what had motivated George the Rude to head for the hills. A man and two women were standing near the van covered in blood, gnawing on what looked suspiciously like human flesh, some of it still covered in blue material. Kinda like the blue a police officer might wear.

"Oh my God," Amberly's voice was strangely calm. *"Tom I hope you all can see this because I can't get to the camera. George, that prick, has run away and left me here alone and now I'm stuck on top of the van. There are three people below me that appear to be. . .what are you looking at?"* Amberly demanded as the three zombies looked up at her, attracted by the sound of her voice. Even as she repeated the demand the man moved to the edge of the van and reached up toward the reporter whose leg was visible in the edge of the picture.

"Stay back!" Amberly was finally getting it I could tell, but it was too late for

her now. *"I mean it, if you don't stay back. .
.I'm a reporter! You can't touch me, I have a
right to be here!"*

I didn't figure that threat would do
much good and I was right. The male
zombie jumped slightly and just missed
grabbing Amberly's leg as she jumped back
off camera to avoid it's grasp.

This was our first real good look at
what Connie and I had both feared to see.
The man had been taller than average it
looked like, wearing a shirt and tie that
were both splattered with blood. His face
was also bloody and his right shoulder
looked as if a chunk had been bitten out of
it. His eyes were slightly glazed looking as
he looked right into the camera for an
instant, following Amberly I guess since we
could hear her moving along the roof in the
background.

"Stay back!" she screamed again. *"Tom,
my God, Tom, I need. . .I need help!
Someone help me!"* There was gunfire now
in the background but with George the
camera man gone there was no one to pan
the camera so we could see what was

happening. We could hear Kelly Amberly screaming until. . .

Suddenly the picture cut back to the studio where 'Tom' was trying to compose himself.

"Well, looks like we lost the live feed from Kelly Amberly," he managed not to stammer too bad. *"We'll try and get that back as soon as possible, but in the meantime let's review the emergency precautions the Health Department has recently released to try and help stop the spre-"* I cut the feed off, looking at Connie over the table.

"Well, that'll stir something up I'd imagine."

*****

I had been right. The 'incident' at Overtown had definitely stirred something up.

We had loaded up and secured the house, then headed into town to the hospital. Connie was no longer protesting my being there, either. Both of us had just experienced a serious wake-up call of our own.

It was one thing to think you knew what was coming. It was another to be confronted with it, knowing that it was literally in your own backyard this time. Videos and stories from Europe, rumors from far away places in other states, these things had caused concern, sure. But they were distant. Distance that made the threat seem a little less real, somehow.

That illusion had been well and truly shattered this morning with an apparent zombie attack just miles from us. Those three we had seen on the camera would not have been the only ones, either. The mere fact that they were standing there unmolested while they munched on what might well have been parts and pieces of a police officer was proof that the other officers had been busy. What could have prevented them from shooting those three? Well, trying not to get eaten themselves was my first guess.

And where the hell was the National Guard? I knew that they had been activated to help with crowd and riot control, but where had they been when the problem at Overtown had flared up?

"Drake," Connie's voice brought me out of my thoughts. I looked at her and found her pointing ahead to. . . .

"Well, that answers that," I murmured to myself as I saw a collection if Humvee trucks at a roadblock just ahead. Several soldiers were manning that roadblock, checking vehicles as they passed each way.

"What?" Connie asked.

"I was just wondering where the Guard was," I told her, slowing. As we approached the roadblock I rolled the window down. At the last second I locked my door and ordered Connie to do the same.

"Why?" she asked as she did so.

"Just a precaution," I shrugged. As I stopped a soldier gave Big Baby an appreciative eye walking to the door.

"State your business," he said flatly. I didn't miss the way he handled his rifle as he spoke.

"I'm doctor Constance Kane," Connie said, leaning over me slightly. Constance, huh? I hadn't realized that. Kinda liked it.

"We're on the way to the hospital. It's my shift in the ER," Connie continued. The soldier behind the questioner consulted a clipboard and then nodded.

"We'll take her from here," the soldier stated.

"No, you won't," I said evenly, moving Connie back slightly. This was not going to happen.

"We're supposed to gather all medical professionals at the hospital, sir," the soldier's hand tightened on his rifle. "Governor's orders."

"Couldn't care less," I informed him. "I'm taking her to the ER, and when the shit gets too deep I'm taking her home, solider. That's not open for negotiation, either. She's here as a volunteer, not a hospital employee. And while I'm sure you guys are doing your best, you'll be concerned with more than her safety. I won't be."

"Sir, that's not how this works," he started but I cut him off.

"It is today," I said simply. "Or we go home. Your call, soldier. I'm good with going home, to be honest."

"I can't allow-"

"You going to shoot me, solider?" I asked calmly, far more calmly than I felt. "Cause that's just what you're going to have to do to separate this woman from me. And you probably won't survive the experience. That's not a threat, it's just the way it is. She's willing to help, even though she's under no obligation to do so. Volunteer, like I said. There is no way I'm leaving her here, in your care or anyone else's. Not. Going. To happen."

Connie was quiet during all this and I worried that she was getting angry at me for the whole 'me Tarzan' act, but this whole thing felt wrong and I wasn't going for it.

"You'll have to proceed at your own risk," the soldier said finally. "We don't have the manpower to escort you."

"I'm her escort," I told him. "Let me worry about her, you worry about whatever it is you guys have to do. Fair enough?"

293

"Be careful," he nodded. "It's crazy. Not just here but everywhere."

"We saw," I nodded. "I'll mind it. You guys be safe," I offered, then rolled up the window as another soldier moved the barricade from across the road. Soon we were rolling, on our way to the hospital. I drove a bit slower than normal. The streets were crazy, cars sitting everywhere and people roaming the street looking a bit worse for wear.

"Thank you," I heard Connie say softly.

"What?" I asked, glancing her way for a second. She looked smaller for some reason, like she'd sank into the seat.

"I said thank you," she spoke a little louder. "I would have gone with them if you'd wanted me to."

"You're delusional if you think I'm letting you out of my sight after what we saw this morning," I snorted. "And while I'm sure those kids are great guys, there's no way I trust them with your safety."

"I know," she nodded. "That's why . . . thank you," she settled for saying again. I reached out and patted her leg gently.

"You don't have to thank me," I told her sincerely. "There's nothing I wouldn't do for you, Constance Kane," I smiled. "And that included shooting soldier-boy back there. I didn't really think it would come to that, but I was prepared to do it."

"I. . .I don't want you to get hurt for me," she said after a minute.

"I wasn't planning on getting hurt, but if I did get hurt, protecting you, that's fine. I can live with it. And if I can, you can too," I winked. She grinned sheepishly but nodded.

"Now enough about that," I told her. "When we get to the hospital I'm going in with you. I'll stay out of the way but I'm going to be nearby. I had originally planned to just be around close but after this morning, I'll be within earshot. All you have to do is sing out and I'll be there."

By way of answer she leaned across the cab and kissed me gently on the cheek. I glanced at her and found her looking at me a little. . .well, not strange, but different.

"Are you okay?" I asked, maybe a little suspiciously.

"I'm fine," she nodded, leaving her hand on my arm as I drove. We made the rest of the trip in silence, her hand never leaving my arm.

I had expected it to be difficult to find parking but that wasn't the case. There was an notable absence of vehicles in the parking lot behind the building where employees parked. Connie removed a placard that said 'Physician' from her bag and hung it on the rear-view mirror. I grabbed my own bag and hit the kill switch before we dismounted.

Connie led the way to the rear entrance and slid a card from her ring down a reader to let us inside. There was a man inside wearing what looked like a janitorial uniform sitting near the door. He jumped to his feet as we entered.

"Doctor Kane," the man smiled. A name-tag on his shirt said 'Ralph'.

"Hello, Ralph," Connie smiled. "How are things?"

"Crazy, Doctor Kane," Ralph admitted. "We're over-run with people this morning and have been for several hours. Days I guess would be more accurate. At least since Monday. I've heard rumors that we're running short of some supplies but of course I don't have any official word of that."

"What are you doing here?" she asked.

"They've assigned non-medical folks to each entrance, I guess to 'guard' the doors," Ralph shrugged. "And to allow employees entrance of course," he added. "My orders are to allow only hospital employees entrance." He looked at me.

"Well, you didn't allow me inside," Connie said firmly. "I have my own key and let myself in, so that's not a problem. And he's with me. *Stays* with me," she added. I said nothing, keeping my face impassive. This was her world, not mine. She was in charge.

"Works for me," Ralph nodded at once. "You need someone to look after you, ma'am. People are crazy, Doctor Kane. I mean *crazy*. We've had several incidents in the ER especially with people demanding drugs and 'the vaccine'. I don't know what vaccine it is, exactly, but some people are certain we have it."

"There's no vaccine for this madness," Connie snorted.

"That's what Doctor Smith said, too," Ralph nodded. "There's a cop at the ER entrance, but they've had to pull him twice for emergencies so I don't know if he's there at the moment or not."

"Well, we'll see I guess," Connie nodded and started walking. "You take care, Ralph."

"You too, Doctor Kane."

I followed Connie around a dizzying array of turns and twists, wondering how anyone found their way anywhere here. I pulled a small crayon from my bag and started making small marks along the wall at each turn. Connie caught me and asked what I was doing.

"Fluorescent marker," I told her, holding the small marker up. "If the lights are out it will reflect light from a flashlight. Help me find my way out if I need it."

"Smart," she nodded, eyebrows raised. "You think you'll need it?"

"Better to have and not need," I shrugged.

"Smarter," she smiled as she pushed a button that opened two mechanical doors. Inside sat the back of the Emergency Room. I'd never seen it from here before.

"Here we are," she sighed. "I'll check in and see what's happening. You can hang out anywhere just be careful not to get in the way of the staff."

"No one will know I'm here," I promised. She smiled at me, kissed my cheek again, and then headed for the desk. I saw a chair and pulled it into a small alcove, out of the way, settling in for the duration.

CHAPTER TWELVE

The duration was longer than I had figured. Well, that's not accurate. I knew how long we'd be there, I just hadn't anticipated how long it would take for the hours to go by. That sounds stupid, doesn't it? What I mean is, the day seemed to just drag by. Sound better?

It wasn't that the ER wasn't busy because it was a madhouse. People everywhere, whining about this and that and something else. Don't get me wrong, there were some serious injuries and sickness as well. Three car wrecks with injuries and I saw at least two kids and one adult with obviously broken bones. I felt bad for all of them. This was not a good time to be laid up or dependent on others for care. Not a good time at all.

Connie was one of only two doctors in the ER that day. The other, an older man named Smith, seemed like an okay guy. He did his share, too. One of the things I had been afraid of was that whoever else was working would shuck a bunch of crap off onto Connie, but Smith didn't.

I couldn't honestly say if the amount of staff was normal because I didn't know what normal would look like. There were several nurses and orderlies (or whatever they call them) running around, and I saw at least three people doing housekeeping duties. You know, changing sheets, mopping, sweeping, that kind of stuff. None of them looked happy to be there, but then it was work, so that in itself made it suck, right?

I had my small tablet with me and opened my reader, settling in to my out-of-the-way spot, looking up from my book every few seconds it seemed to keep an eye out. I made it a point to always know what room Connie was in while not hovering or being in the way. That's not as easy as it sounds, either. The ER was pretty big and busy as hell. But, you do what you have to, right?

One thing that probably made the day pass so slow for me was there was a clock right across from my chair. Every time I looked up I could see what time it was whether I really wanted to or not. Usually I didn't, at least not when I realized that maybe two minutes had passed in the last half-hour. Yes, that's sarcasm.

Other than being busy, and loud, things didn't seem to bad for a while. I watched the others and while they looked tired and maybe a bit rushed they didn't look alarmed. That all changed right about lunch time. I was just getting into *The Murders in the Rue Morgue* when I heard someone yelling around the corner from the nurse's station. It was a man's voice. I frowned but stayed put for another few seconds, thinking that it wasn't my place to just run around and see what was happening. Then I heard a woman's scream. It wasn't Connie but it was a scream. I set Mister Poe aside (actually I put my tablet back in my EDC) and walked as casually as I could manage around the station to see what the fuss was. I was careful to stay out of the way since I wasn't supposed to be there and I was going to be exactly no help in a medical emergency.

As soon as I got into the opposite hallway I knew there was a problem, and probably what it was. A woman was sitting in a chair with what looked like a bloody towel wrapped around her lower left leg. There was a fairly large man hovering over the nurse attempting to look at the wound.

"I said she needs the vaccine!" he shouted at the nurse. "Now get it!"

"Sir, I don't even know what's wrong with her," the nurse tried to remain calm. "And what vaccine?"

"Don't give me that shit!" he yelled back. "I saw it on the internet! There's a vaccine for this shit and you're holding for yourselves! Now give it to her!"

"Sir," Connie came out of the room next to where all this was taking place, closing the curtain behind her, "there is no vaccine. None of us have it, this hospital doesn't have it, and so far as I'm aware there isn't one available anywhere. If you'll let us triage your wife, we can see what's wrong and what we can do to help."

"That's a lie!" the woman screeched. "It's all over the internet that the vaccine is being held by the elite! They're just waiting for enough of us to die that it will depopulate the planet!"

Oh boy. Nut cases. I'd read about these for years and even read some blog and forum entries by some of them. I'd never seen any in real life though. Until now.

"Well, if the elite has it, that should tell you that we don't," Connie replied calmly. "None of us rank that high, I'm afraid. As for the internet, that's not really a reliable source of information sometimes. We don't have a vaccine of any kind, but we can treat your injury *if* you'll let us examine it."

"No!" the woman shrieked again, jerking her leg away from the nurse. The nurse stepped back, obviously having had enough.

"I don't get paid enough for this," she said simply and walked away. Connie waved for the woman in the reception window and then pointed toward the door. I could see the woman nod in reply but had no idea what was going on. I wasn't up on ER sign language.

About ten seconds later a policeman came through the door, explaining what the signs had been about.

"What's the problem?" he asked tiredly. He looked like he'd been working far too long and with way too little sleep.

"The lady is refusing treatment and both are demanding access to medicines we don't have," Connie said simply. "We need them removed so we can treat people who want to be treated. We've made every accommodation we can and it's not enough. The staff are afraid and threatening to leave. They have to go."

"Let's move, folks," the officer said to the couple. "Outside to the waiting room. Maybe if you calm down the doctor will see you later on. Give you another chance." He looked at Connie for confirmation but she just shook her head.

"I'll have to see," she finally replied.

"We're not leaving," the man was seething, "until she," he pointed to what I was assuming was his wife, "gets the vaccine." With that he reached behind him. The cop had obviously been expecting that because about two seconds later the man was on the floor with the cop's gun to his head. I have to admit, I was impressed. For a tired guy that was short on sleep he was fast.

"That was a stupid thing to do, sir," the cop almost snarled. He had wrenched the gun from the guy's hand and I could have sworn I heard bones breaking. Served the guy right. And you know, I don't mean to be unfair about that. I know the guy was worried about his wife, or girlfriend, or whatever. But come on, man. You can't just storm into a place with an attitude when you need help like that. And let's face it; the *internet*? Now there is a fountain of truth in a sea of lies, right? Remember that stupid commercial? The one with the blonde who was saying how you couldn't put anything on the internet that wasn't true? Yeah, that's not a real thing, you know.

This guy apparently hadn't gotten that memo.

The woman suddenly came alive and attacked the cop, leaping from her seat and wrapping her arms around his neck, trying to take the officer down the floor. I moved to help him but by the time I had taken two steps Connie had stepped in and landed a hay-maker on the woman's jaw, sending her careening into the wall behind the door to the ER.

That move put her leg where Vaccine Guy could grab her though, and he did, trying to wiggle free of the officer at the same time. Connie tried to kick loose but the guy managed to get his other arm free of the cop's grasp and locked both hands around her ankle, trying to pull her down.

Now I just couldn't have that.

I covered the distance in about three steps. Rather than try and pry the dude's hands loose I just kicked him in the left elbow, the one nearest me. Really hard.

I heard the bone and joint when it gave way but. . .okay, I admit it. Seeing him grab my woman (me Tarzan, right?) kind of aggravated me. . .oh, hell, I was so mad I could have bit a ten-penny nail in two. So I might have kicked his now wrecked elbow again.

Two or three times. Hey, it's easy to lose count when you're upset. Anyway, regardless of how many times I kicked him, he screamed a lot and let go of Connie. I immediately pulled her away from Vaccine Guy's stupid ass and then, just for good measure, kicked him again in the jaw. Wasn't really aiming for his jaw, just, you know, his head in general, but I did hear another satisfying crunch when the toe of my boot hit his jaw. I should be ashamed of doing that, shouldn't I?

Yeah, well I 'm not. Sue me. He grabbed my woman. Tried to hurt her. He started it.

"Are you okay?" I asked her, seeing the look on Connie's face.

"I'm fine," she nodded but a but shakily.

"Get someone to look at your leg while I help this guy," I told her. She looked like she was about to argue but for some reason thought better of it I guess and nodded. I helped her into a chair and grabbed a nurse.

"Make sure she's not injured," I ordered. The guy nurse looked at me, bobbing his head up and down like one of those bobble head dolls. I turned back to the scene on the floor.

And trouble.

The woman was coming around and I could tell things were going from bad to worse. Her eyes were glazing over and there was a blood stain on the wall behind her where her head had hit the wall. Not good.

"Get outta there, man!" I shouted at the cop. Looking past him I saw the receptionist standing there with the door open.

"Get inside and close the door!" I shouted. I don't know if she realized what was happening or was just scared of me but she did it, slamming the door and locking it. The cop was still working on cuffing Vaccine Guy.

"Forget him for a minute and get the hell outta there!" I shouted. "Behind you! Move!" Give the guy his due, he didn't look, he just moved, leaving one cuff on Vaccine Guy's good arm and stumbling toward me. I caught him and helped him straighten up.

"Look," I said softly, pointing to the chick. She was moving now and the look on her face was eerily reminiscent of the three people we had seen on television that morning.

"Dude, she's got the thing!" I hissed to the cop, trying to keep my voice down. "We can't let her bite anyone!"

"What?" the cop looked dazed for a second but then focused. "Shit, you're right!" He drew his Taser and gave her both barrels. He nailed her with both darts, hit the trigger and held it, lighting her ass up good.

Might as well just waved at her. I knew as soon as the Taser didn't work she was gone. The towel was coming off her leg as she crawled toward Vaccine Guy and I could see the ugly bite on her right calf.

"She's bit!" I told the cop. "That's not gonna work." I drew my gun out of pure instinct and fear and the cop looked a bit panicked at the action.

"Hey, man, I'm not trying to do your job, just looking after me and mine," I told him, backing up a bit. "But you're gonna have to put her down before she-"

Even as I said it Towel Girl drew her head back and tore a chunk out of Vaccine Guy's shoulder. He was screaming already from where somebody had sort of ruined his elbow. I don't know how he was managing to babble at his old lady after somebody had broke his jaw but he was trying to talk to her when she nailed him.

"'a'y, 'ease, oo no 'e! Lo!" Which I interpreted to mean 'Baby please, you know me. No.' Not sure of that, of course. Could have been something else. Hard to tell, you know? And whatever it was, it didn't stop her from biting his ass over and over again.

"Man, you gotta shoot her!" I told him, backing up another step. The cop looked lost, but I could tell he'd been briefed on what to do. He drew his gun but hesitated. I started hoping at that point that he'd wait until she killed Vaccine Guy so we could get rid of him, too. I know, I know, that's a horrible thing to think or say, but. . .he was bit, man. Gone. If she didn't kill him then they'd want him to be treated, which meant he'd turn or. . .whatever, right there in the hospital in front of God and everybody, which would just be bad all the way around, you know?

The shot caught me off guard. I wasn't paying attention to the officer and suddenly Towel Girl's head snaps back with a spray of blood and brains all over the wall and she collapses on top of Vaccine Guy. I looked at the cop who was looking at them, a stunned expression on his face. I could tell by looking at him that he'd just experienced a moment of clarity, so to speak. I holstered my own weapon and turned to check on Connie. Nurse guy was looking at her leg.

"There's no broken skin but she'll probably have some bruises," the guy told me. His name tag said 'Mark'. Mark seemed like an okay guy. He was still on the job despite everything. Including a shooting not twenty feet from him.

"Thanks, Mark," I nodded. Connie was starting to shake a bit and I figured it was shock, maybe.

"I need to get her a blanket, and maybe get her out of the hallway," Mark told me. "I'll take her to room Five, okay?" he pointed to the room just down the hall from where we were. I nodded and he helped her up and led her toward the room. She looked back at me and I smiled, lifting a hand to wave.

"It's okay, Connie," I told her. "I'll be right there, okay?" She nodded at me and went into the room. I turned back to where the cop was using his cell phone. I started toward Vaccine Guy, I guess thinking I'd check to see if he was dead. Or undead. Or well, whatever, but the cop stopped me.

"Don't," he ordered, his voice calm once again. "Orders are not to touch anyone who might be infected and don't get blood on you." He looked down at himself, checking. I looked at his back, but couldn't see anything. Since blood might not show up on Navy blue I looked for dark or wet spots but didn't see anything.

"I think you're good, man," I told him. "Why don't you grab a chem shower," I pointed to the room next to us, "and get them to bring you some scrubs. Get out of that uniform just in case."

"Yeah, good idea," he nodded. "I gotta call this in, first."

"Who to?" I asked, curious.

"Guard has a medical unit on standby for this shit. Just a couple guys, but. . .this wasn't supposed to happen here. We were supposed to be clean."

"I'd wager they were in the city last night," I reminded him of what had happened that morning. "She might have been bitten there and they couldn't get her in to see a doctor. Course he was pretty adamant about that vaccine thing, too," I added.

"Is there a vaccine?" he asked quietly, fear registering in his eyes.

"Not that I've heard," I admitted. "But it was on the 'net according to him," I nodded at Vaccine Guy.

"Oh, well that makes it true then, don't it?" the cop muttered. He seemed like he had a clue, this guy. His name tag said 'Jacobs'.

"That's what I thought Officer Jacobs," I nodded.

"Ham," he told me. "Hamilton Jacobs, but everyone calls me Ham."

"Shelton Drake, but everyone just calls me Drake," I introduced myself.

"The guy from the pizza shooting?" his eyebrows rose.

"Uh, maybe," I replied warily.

"Good shoot," he nodded then turned away as someone finally answered his call.

"This is Jacobs, ER," he said tersely. "We've got one positive and one possible, a victim that was with the positive. He's been bitten by the positive." Pause. "No, the positive is dead. Head shot. We haven't been near the possible since he was bitten." Pause. "What about the patients?" Pause. "That should work. I'll get on it." He shut his phone, then opened it again and dialed another number.

"I need you to bring my ready bag to the ER," he said into the phone. Pause. "Because I need it numb nuts," he growled. Pause. "Look, will you go and get my damn bag and bring it to me? I've. . .I've had an incident. I need fresh clothes." Pause. "Thanks, man." He closed the phone again and put it away.

"We'll have to leave that door shut off," he told me. "I'll have to find another way for people to get in here for treatment."

"I, ah, I don't really know anything about that," I admitted. "I'm just here to keep an eye on the doctor."

"An eye on her?" he asked.

"Making sure nothing happens to her," I added. He nodded in understanding then and grinned.

"Lucky bastard," he told me, without rancor. "Look, can you get someone to open another route in here? I'd really like to get that shower and ditch this outfit. Guard unit is on the way."

"I find someone," I promised. "Go ahead." I turned away and headed for the nurse's station but halted at his call.

"Drake?" I turned look back at him.

"Thanks, man," Jacobs said. "I appreciate it."

"No problem, man," I nodded. I got to the nurse's station to find them in a mild state of pandemonium.

"Excuse me, folks," I interrupted the gaggle. "Officer Jacobs says we'll need to route patients through another door until the. . .scene is cleaned. Is there another way in here that we can use from the waiting area?" They all looked at me dumbly for a few seconds.

"Seriously, folks," I urged and one of the older women seemed to shake loose.

"We can bring them around the reception and through the rear hallway," she told me, pointing.

"Can you inform the receptionist of that by phone?" I asked. "She really needs to stay put for the moment unless there's another way out of that office."

"There is, but I'll call her," the woman nodded. "Is Connie okay?" she asked.

"Seems like it," I nodded. "I'm going now to see. Officer Jacobs is in the chem shower but he needs a set of scrubs to wear. He's got new clothes on the way but it may be a few minutes."

"I'll get them," a younger woman rose, finally galvanized into action. "We've got to get things back under control around here," she said to herself more than us.

"Look, I think this was an isolated thing," I said, hoping I was right. "I think those two were in the city last night and that's how she got bit. Still, keep sharp and be looking."

"Are you going to be here?" the older woman asked as she picked up the phone.

"As long as Doctor Kane is, yes," I left it at that and moved to room Five, looking down the hallway at Vaccine Guy's body to make sure he was still dead. Or at least down.

He was.

Connie was lying on the bed, Mark taking her blood pressure.

"That's not necessary," she told him. "I'm not sick, I scared."

"All the more reason to check your vitals," Mark smiled. "Besides, it gives me something to do."

"How you doing?" I asked, taking her other hand in mine. She squeezed my hand

and smiled at me. It was a little weak, but that was understandable as far as I was concerned.

"Thank you," she almost whispered.

"My job," I winked at her and she blushed ever so slightly.

"Looks okay," Mark said, unhooking the cuff. "You should wait in here until you've got your equilibrium back," he told her. "Looks like we'll be out of business for a few minutes, anyway."

"A few," I agreed. "Clean up is on the way. Make sure no one goes near those two, and if he moves you call me. Jacobs, Officer Jacobs," I corrected, "is cleaning up and then he'll be back."

"Will do," Mark nodded and left, pulling the curtain over the door as he did so. I used my free hand to move Connie's hair from her face and she looked up at me.

"I. . .I was afraid," she told me.

"Hell, so was I," I said truthfully. "That was a hell of a hay-maker you laid out lady," I told her, smiling. "Nice punch."

"I didn't even think about it," she admitted. "I should have."

"You probably saved Jacobs," I told her. "Quick thinking, baby. I don't think I'd have gotten there in time."

"Baby?" she asked, eyebrow rising.

"I didn't think you'd approve of Doctor Hottie here in the ER," I whispered as I bent lower and kissed her lightly. She smothered a laugh.

"I'd rather you didn't," she admitted. "I'm okay, really, just shaken up." She went to raise up and I helped her.

"I need to get up," she told me. "I can't lay here or I'll fall apart. I have to get back on my feet."

"Okay," I nodded. "Tell me what I can do."

"You can hold me, just for a minute," she admitted and I enveloped her in a hug. She felt fragile for once and I hated that. I was afraid this was going to hurt her confidence in herself and that was the last thing I wanted to see.

"Thank you," she said again, her voice muffled against my chest. "I'm saying that a lot to you today," she looked up at me.

"You never have to say it," I told her simply.

"That just makes it more important that I do," she smiled a little. "Now," she straightened. "I need to get back to work." She rose to her feet and was once more Doctor Hottie. Calm, cool, composed.

"I'll just be out of the way," I nodded. She touched my cheek gently for a second.

"You're never in the way."

Aw, heck.

*****

The two-man Guard team arrived about ten minutes later wearing some kind of modified MOPP gear. They entered through the original entrance even as patients were being brought through the rear hallway. Jacobs was in scrubs, his uniform placed in a bio-hazard bag for disposal. As we watched the Guard guys removed the two bodies, another cop came in through the ambulance entrance with a duffel bag.

"Ham!" he called out, and Jacobs turned just in time to catch the tossed bag.

"Gotta go, man!" the guy called over his shoulder as he was already heading back out. "Shooting at Wal-Mart. Be sharp!" Jacobs lowered the bag, shaking his head.

"I don't know him much further we can go," he muttered. "You watch things while I change, Drake?" he asked me.

"Sure thing, dude," I nodded. "It's just letting the Guard guys do their thing right now anyway."

"I'll be back in five," he said as he moved away to find a place to gear up again. I noticed Connie talking to Mark and another nurse before ducking into another exam room. Mark headed by me and I stopped him with a hand to his arm.

"She okay?" I asked softly.

"She's good," he promised. "That's a tough woman, man. I've seen soldiers not deal that well."

"Your service?" I asked.

"Once upon," he smiled and nodded. "Where I got my degree. Almost wish I was still there and yet glad I'm not. Know what I mean?"

"I get you," I said. "Thanks, man."

"What I do," Mark assured me and moved on about his business. That explained his calmness, I figured. Dude was a combat vet. All in a day's work for him.

Me, not so much. This had been a hell of a week for me so far. Wasn't anything I could do about it though.

The Guard duo came back and got Vaccine Guy, loading him onto another stretcher. One of them checked him.

"He's got a pulse," I heard the muffled statement from twenty feet away. "Let's get him out of here." The two moved away with a little quicker step. I was under no illusions that Vaccine Guy was going to get medical treatment. If he was lucky he'd get a bullet to the head. Jacobs got back just as the two left with Vaccine Guy. He was wearing a black tactical outfit now, complete with thigh holster and web gear.

"Thanks, Drake," he told me. "I got it."

"Sure thing, Ham," I nodded. "They just got Vaccine Guy out. One of 'em said he had a pulse. No idea what they're doing with him."

"I don't want to know," Ham shrugged. "I really don't. You gonna be around?" he asked.

"Long as Doctor Kane is, yeah," I nodded.

"Keep your eyes open," he told me. "I need another set of eyes. Long as you're here and don't mind, I can use the help."

"You got it," I promised.

CHAPTER THIRTEEN

You know, time sure flies when you're having fun.

And it drags like a stick in your shoe laces when you ain't.

By two o'clock I was so bored I could have cried. I mean seriously cried, just for some kind of tension relief. But that would have been unmanly and all, so I had to suck it up. I had pitched in here and there to help out, but mostly I just stayed out of the way.

There hadn't been any more 'scares' since Vaccine Guy and Towel Girl- I really need to quit calling them that, but thing is I never got their names. Not sure anyone did. Anyway. There hadn't been anything else like that and no one in to get a bite treated. After them it was just standard ER stuff, though maybe a bit more of it. Part of that I figured was because so many doctor's offices, like Connie's, were closed. That left the ER.

Jacobs kept order pretty well the few times someone acted up. It wasn't often, and even then it was usually an irate parent angry that 'little Billy' wasn't getting treated fast enough or that 'little Millie' should have been seen ahead of 'Little Billy', that kind of crap. People were scared, that's all. Add the fear of the end of the world to the fear of a sick of hurt child and there you go. Instant problems.

As three o'clock rolled nearer and nearer I saw Connie and Doctor Smith in a hushed little conversation near the nurse's station. As they were talking a middle aged woman with a face that only a mother or a man after money could really love walked up to them, hands on her hips and an angry look on her face.

I decided that I had now seen 'Madeline' the hospital administrator.

There was a quiet but animated discussion that involved some finger pointing, some other hand gestures, and from the way Madeline's face flushed at least a little bit of name calling. I couldn't hear what was being said and Connie hadn't motioned me over so I sat still and watched.

At one point Jacobs was called over and Madeline began talking to him. He stood there about fifteen seconds and then shook his head at the overbearing woman and walked away, leaving her in a huff and leaving Connie and Smith gloating just a bit. Finally 'Madeline' stalked away and Connie walked over to where I was sitting.

"Guess what?" she asked tiredly, sitting beside me for a minute.

"The night shift doctors aren't coming and she's trying to make you and Smith stay," I guessed. "She tried to get Jacobs to back her and he refused. I'm guessing you and Smith both decided to stay for half the next shift and she's got to try and get the late night people in here by then. How's that?"

By that point her eyes were as wide as they could probably get and her mouth was making a little 'O' of amazement. Hey, sometimes I am amazing, you know?

"How in the world did you know any of that?" she finally managed to ask.

"All lucky guesses," I admitted. "I haven't seen her in here all day, she suddenly shows up at quitting time talking to you two and both of you look mad. Judging by her face at times neither of you were very nice to her, and she tried to get Jacobs to use his 'po'leece' authority to make you stay on the job. He pretty much told her to kiss his ass and went back to work at which point the two of you spoke to each other like she wasn't there then said something short to her. She storms out and now here you are asking 'guess what?' That pretty much covers it," I finished, feigning disinterest. Honestly I was disappointed that we weren't going home, but it was her call, not mine.

"Amazing," she shook her head. "Right down to Smith calling her a dictator and me calling her a shrew," she laughed.

"Looks like it fits," I nodded. "Well, I guess I should see if I can round us up something to eat if we're going to be here a while longer. Give me some choices I can make for you depending on what's available. Smith too, if he's hungry. I'll check with Jacobs."

"You aren't mad are you?" she asked, biting her lip just a little.

"Of course not," I scoffed. "No reason to be. You're a doctor. You'd never leave all these people with no one to care for them. One of the reasons I love you."

I said it before I thought. In fact I wasn't thinking. I could tell right away that I'd either said something very right or completely wrong. Isn't it funny how that line is so small? So thin?

Connie's eyes widened slightly and a flush hit her cheeks.

"Ah, I didn't mean to startle you there," I said into the gulf of silence. "Or upset you, if it did," I added when she didn't say anything. "Uh, Connie?" I asked, resisting the urge to run away.

"I. . . ." she started, but then stopped. I could tell she was struggling to come up with something. I knew how she felt.

"Look, I'm sorry," I said gently. "I swear I wasn't trying to-"

"It's okay," she smiled suddenly, almost shyly. "Don't be sorry, either," she added, moving to where I stood. She eased up on her tiptoes and kissed me just a little.

"You know what? I'll take a cheeseburger and fries if you can scrounge me one up," she whispered. "And a Coke."

"Done deal," I nodded. "Check with Smith and I'll talk to Ham and then go get us something."

"Okay," she nodded and went to ask her associate what he might want to eat. I found Jacobs standing at the entrance of the ER, looking out at the waiting room.

"Hey man," I said softly. "We're staying another few hours, looks like," I told him.

"Yeah, I know," he nodded, his eyes never leaving the waiting room. "Man it's a mess out there," he sighed.

"I'm going to see about rummaging up something to eat. You want anything?" He finally looked at me then.

"You think anything will be open?"

"No idea, but if I'm extremely lucky Jacks is still open because I seriously need a Big Jack," I grinned.

"I'll take two," he laughed. "And two fries, but without that cheesy junk they put on them," he added, reaching for his wallet.

"I know, right? My treat man," I waved his hand off. "I'm collecting for Connie and Doctor Smith, too. I'll be back when I can. I assume as long as I can find you something dead in bread, it'll be okay?"

"Suits," he nodded. "Man you really need to be careful out there. It's bad and getting worse."

"I'll watch it," I agreed. I left him to find Connie waiting for me.

"Doctor Smith said he'd take a burger as well," she grinned. "Since it's the end of the world why not load up on fast food."

"Sounds like a smart man," I nodded firmly. "Okay, I'm off to see what I can dig up. You watch yourself until I get back."

"You watch yourself, mister," she pushed a finger into my chest in warning. "You'll be out among all that crazy."

"I'll be very careful," I promised. "I have every reason to be safe and come back unharmed," I winked. She blushed slightly and kissed me lightly again. She slipped me her key card so I could get myself in and out the back door and off I went, into the Zombie Apocalypse.

*****

I had actually meant that to be funny, but once I was outside and on the move, things really did look bad. I mean, not actual, real life Zombie Apocalypse bad, at least not yet, but . . . saying town looked like a war zone, at least in places, wasn't really inaccurate. There were fires in at least three places judging by the smoke columns, some looting on a small scale here and there, I saw at least four fist fights and three groups of armed citizens who were clearly standing guard over their stores or neighborhoods. And that was all in a five block range. The last block was back to the highway which is where I saw most of the criminal activity and the smoke. Shaking my head I turned onto the street and eased toward my favorite heart attack in a bag joint. Hey, what's the point of being hooked up with a doctor if you don't live a little badly right?

Anyway. The situation had deteriorated a good bit since we'd arrived this morning. The further from the hospital I got the worse it looked. I saw a few police but they were all running somewhere with lights and sirens. I saw two ambulances and knew that it would be a while before Connie got to eat, assuming I found her anything.

Most of the stores that had been open this morning were closed, including all but two of the around-the-clock variety. Both were out of gas or I would have tried to fill up. True, I had fuel at home and Big Baby was still mostly full, but an ounce of prevention, right?

I was starting to worry that nothing would be open when I spied one plucky C-Store owner who was still trying. He had a drive through window which was just awesome and I pulled up to it.

"You got cash?" he demanded through the speaker.

"Well, that depends," I smiled. "You got change?" and held up a twenty. He nodded and opened the window.

I bought eight Cokes and eight more Powerades of various flavors. Or colors, depending on how you looked at it.

"How long you gonna try to hang on?" I asked, wondering if he'd be here for another run if I had to make one."

"Maybe sundown," he admitted. "It's dangerous now and getting worse by the minute. I'm going to leave before dusk and hopefully get home before it's completely dark. I doubt I'll be back to be honest."

"Can't say I blame you," I admitted. "If that's the case, let me get that order again, just in case," I said, handing over more money. Soon I had a seat full of soft drinks and was ready to look for something to eat.

"Good luck," I told the guy and he waved as I drove off. I hoped he made it.

Back on the highway I made my way down to the intersection and saw that the Jacks sign was lit up. That was not a guarantee that I would be getting a burger, but it was encouraging. I narrowly avoided being hit by a soccer man in a soccer van as I pulled into the parking lot, with her showing me her long middle finger as her opinion of my driving. It apparently didn't occur to mom of the year that A) her kids were in the back seat watching, and B) she was the one at fault.

Road rage was never one of my weaknesses and I let if slide away. I had so much bigger fish to fry. I mean, so to speak.

Bless capitalism in all it's hedonistic forms. Jacks was indeed open for business the cheery voice behind the magic box informed me. I gleefully ordered two burgers for everyone else and three for me, eight orders of fries sans 'cheesy salt' (that crap really is awful) and at the last minute added a fried pie for everyone. What the hell, right?

I pulled to the window and paid, waiting patiently for my cholesterol destroying goodies while surfing the radio.

In a movie, this would have been the part where some thug came up and tried to steal my truck and I shot/stabbed/punched/ran over him. Lucky for me this wasn't a movie because I am not an action hero, and no miscreant appeared. Soon I was being handed bag after bag of decadent deliciousness.

"How long will you guys try to stay open?" I asked. Need-to-know information right there.

"Until the food's gone," the manager shrugged. "There's no reason not to keep serving, since it looks like we won't get more any time soon and I expect orders to close up shop any time. But as long as I've got someone to help me and we've got food. . .well, people have to eat. We're feeding the cops, firemen and paramedics for free."

"Damn, I wish I had known that," I laughed. "I just bought for the cop and two doctors at the ER."

"If you come back, I'll remember you," he promised. "If we're still serving, the next one will be on me."

"That's pretty cool of you, man," I nodded my thanks. "You guys be careful though. People are crazy out here. Could get dangerous in a hurry."

"There's me and three others and we're all armed," he informed me. "Against store policy, but. . .I've seen the videos. What are they gonna do? Fire me?"

"Sure enough," I nodded. "Take care and be careful."

"You too," he nodded then closed and locked the window. Another good guy. Seemed like the good folks always came out in bad times, you know?

The trip back was anti-climactic to say the least. I had expected trouble everywhere, but that wasn't the case. I mean there was trouble everywhere don't get me wrong, but none of it directed at me which was what I was worried about.

I had been gone well less than an hour when I parked Baby again behind the hospital and managed, somehow, to get all those sacks to the door. I had to swipe Connie's card three times to get the door to open but finally staggered in the door with my purchases. Making sure the door was closed I made the long trip back through the hallway maze to the ER.

I could see I had been right about the ambulances as people were running back and forth from four different rooms that had been empty when I left. Avoiding the scurrying staff by keeping well out of their way, I found a small office that the doctors used to write up reports sitting empty and placed all the sacks on the desk or in a chair. I got Jacobs' attention and waved him over, offering him the right bag and a Coke.

"Oh, man that looks good," he rubbed his hands together. "Sure I can't pay you?"

"Cops are eating free at Jacks," I shook my head, lying just a little. Guy was working his ass off. It didn't hurt me to be nice to him.

"All it took was the end of the world," he chuckled. "I can sit here in the door and keep watch I guess," he said to no one in particular, dragging a chair over to the doorway. I watched for Connie for a minute but didn't see her. I did see Mark the combat nurse and made my way to him.

"Know where Doctor Kane is?" I asked him.

"Room Six," he replied without looking up from the bed he was working on. "Car wreck. Pretty bad. Soccer mom and two kids hit a semi."

Nah, no way. I'd seen the ambulances before I'd seen the mom from hell. I shook it off and went back to the office. Connie would eat she she could. I unwrapped one of mine and started eating. I was extremely hungry.

"I had no idea how hungry I was," Jacobs informed me as he stuffed a half-dozen fries in his mouth. "I don' thin' I a'e all da'," he added and I nodded as if I understood him. I was pretty sure he said "I don't think I ate all day," but. . .I've been wrong before.

As I ate I thought about something the C-Store guy had said. Home before dark. I started thinking about what time it got dark, then about what time Connie would be free to leave assuming a four hour extension, adjusted for daylight savings time, carried the one and realized with a start that it would be nearly an hour after dark before we even *left* the hospital.

And there went my appetite.

*****

I should go ahead and admit here that I ate my burgers anyway. No way was I letting them go to waste. You might think I was getting tired of them but you would be completely wrong. There was nothing better so far as I was concerned, at least when it came to fast food. Sonic ran a close second, but it was still second in my opinion.

It was nearly thirty minutes before Connie and Doctor Smith had the chance to come and eat. Both looked drawn and near exhaustion. Both sat down at the small desk and tore into the food.

"What do I owe you?" Smith asked.

"Nothing," I waved it away. "Money may not be any good before the day's out, and anyway Jacks in feeding cops, firemen and paramedics for free. Manager said he'd add ER folks too. Well, doctors anyway," I amended. No sense in creating a rush and I didn't know that they would feed nurses free. I should have asked I guess.

"I appreciate it," he nodded, eating his food on auto-pilot.

"The mother may survive," Connie said suddenly, her voice a little numb sounding.

"Possible," he nodded absently. "May wish she hadn't once she realizes her children didn't make it. According to the paramedics the wreck was her fault."

I made myself a promise right then that I wasn't going to go and look into that. If it was the same woman, I didn't want to know. I hadn't wished anything bad on her, but. . .I don't know. It just seemed like I didn't want to know. Does that make sense?

Anyway.

"We've got another two hours before the midnight shift should be coming in," Connie said, bringing up a subject that we were all avoiding. Namely, what would the two of them do if they doctors didn't come in like they were supposed to?

"I've got children at home," Smith shrugged. "I've done all I can do and I have to think of my own family at some point." He was almost defensive but I didn't see a reason for it. He was right, you know? His family had to take precedence in something like this. He wouldn't be much of a dad if his kids didn't come first. My opinion of him rose another notch.

"I don't have any children but I'm exhausted," Connie admitted. "I'll be back in the morning," she said then looked at me. I nodded quietly. If she wanted to come back I'd see to it she got here if I could.

"But I'm leaving when my time is up," she finished after I nodded. "I don't want to be out after dark and I'm not staying here all night. Tired doctors make mistakes."

"I saw Patrick a few minutes ago," Smith offered. "I know he wasn't here earlier, so he's probably going to work the late shift. At least there will be a P.A. As far as tomorrow, I don't know," he shook his head. "If my family is safe then yeah, I'll probably come back at least one more day. But that's all I'm willing to promise. And that depends on my family's safety, like I said."

"I don't think we're being bad people, or doctors," Connie said, almost as if trying to reassure herself.

"Hey, is that Madeline. . .person, a doctor?" I asked suddenly.

"She used to be," Smith snorted. "She's become a bureaucrat since she took over the hospital."

"Well, she can pretend to be one again and work the night shift then," I said firmly. The two of them looked at me, then looked at each other and suddenly broke into laughter.

"They'd be better off with a witch doctor," Smith laughed. "Seriously. She hasn't seen a real patient in. . .I don't even know how long," he finished after the pause to think. "Six, seven years at least."

"Can't see where that's your fault," I said simply.

"It's not, but it's a hard decision," he admitted. "Still, I can't call myself much of a father if I don't take care of my own children."

"No question," I nodded.

"Well, we better get back and check on things," Connie stood. "The mom's scan should be done by now. I'm sure she needs surgery, but how much I don't know."

"And there's no surgeon here," Smith nodded grimly. "I'm sure they're calling someone, but if I was safe at home and it getting close to dark? My phone would probably not be on."

"I always check my voice mail first thing every morning," I laughed.

The two of them were still chuckling as they filed out to return to the business of sick and injured people. I had tried to make them laugh and I had. I hoped it was enough.

The rest of the afternoon was pretty uneventful considering that the situation outside was deteriorating steadily. Wow, that sounded like a sound-bite for a news program didn't it? What I meant to say was that the world outside was going to hell on a Slip-n-Slide coated with vegetable oil.

Connie's original shift was seven to three. Typical day shift hours in most places I guess. She and Smith had agreed to stay for another half-shift, which would place us leaving at seven that evening. I didn't want us to be out after dark like that but there wasn't much to do about it. If this happened tomorrow though I didn't know that I wouldn't argue with her about staying that late. Maybe work six in the morning to six in the evening, or something like that. We'd have the light most of the day.

It wasn't that I minded being at the hospital at night. That wasn't it. But I didn't want the house setting there empty even with the alarm. Not to mention the fact that no matter how careful you were, you were vulnerable in the failing light. If someone was casing the hospital they would see us come and go. If they were casing the house, they could hit us at the gate coming or going.

I knew there was no way to eliminate the risks but we *could* minimize them, right? When you're in a potential war zone, you change the way you do things to accommodate that kind of situation. You can't count on police protection any more, you can't count on any emergency services for that matter. You damn sure can't count on human kindness because when it looks like the end of the world, there ain't no human kindness. There's just people who will do anything to survive.

It doesn't matter to some people that you worked hard to have what you have. The fact is you have it, they need it, so it's only 'fair' that you hand it over. And there are people out there that will 'sympathize' with the thief. You will note however that the libtards who are advocating for the 'distressed and under-privileged' have never been the victim of said distressed and under-privileged thugs. How many times did you see where some person famous for anti-gun advocacy had shot a home invader, or been found in possession of an illegal weapon. But that was *different*. Why? Because it was *them*, that's why.

It wasn't personal but I worked hard to make sure I was prepared. On top of that I now had Connie to worry about taking care of. If she reads that she'll probably hit me, but that's what happens, man. You care about someone and you start worrying about taking care of them, you know?

And that meant making sure nothing happened to her. Or to my ability to take care of her, either. Circular thinking brings me back to it's safer if we aren't out in the world after dark. But there was no way around it for today. It would be dark before we could leave, and that was assuming we left at seven. Connie had sounded firm about going home, but I knew how dedicated she was so there was the chance that she would agree to stay longer. If she did I would stay with her, but I really didn't want us to. In the end it would be up to her.

At least it was supposed to be.

*****

"Hey man, you got a minute?" Jacobs asked quietly. "Need to talk to you in private." I looked at him quizzically but followed him to an empty exam room.

"Listen, things are about to get intense in a few minutes," he said softly, looking through the door as if to see if anyone was listening in. "That troll that runs the hospital has managed to get someone to sign off on an order to keep your doctor and all the other staff working whether they want to or not."

"That can't even approach being legal," I objected.

"It's not, but who's going to say so?" he shrugged. "I owe you man, so I'm giving you a heads up. You didn't get this from me. You got about ten minutes before the order comes down. Tops."

"Thanks, Ham," I nodded. "Be safe, brother," I added.

"Good luck," he nodded and offered his hand. We shook and then he was gone, back to the door. I waited half-a-minute before going straight to where Connie was finishing a chart.

"Get your things," I told her softly. "We're leaving, right now. We've got about ten minutes before they lock this place down tight to prevent you, any of you, from leaving." Her eyes widened as the import of what I'd said hit her.

"I have to tell Smith," she said finally. "He has children."

"Do the rest of them?" I asked, waving around the room. She paused.

"I don't know," she admitted. "I don't know many of them that well."

"You can tell him but be ready to hit the door when you do," I told her. "I'm not leaving here without you and I'm not about to leave you here with this crowd. It's too dangerous at this point."

"Okay," she nodded and hurried away, catching Smith as he emerged from an exam room. I hadn't told her where I got my information and I had my tablet in hand so she might assume that I'd seen it in the news. I didn't want Ham in trouble over this. I saw Smith's face cloud up and then he was moving. Connie came back to where I was waiting, stopping by the small office to grab her bag. Before anyone was the wiser we were at the back door.

Ralph was gone but there was another guy sitting there, reading.

"Sorry Doctor Kane," he said, standing. "No one's allowed to leave through this door."

"Sorry Pete, but we parked back here," Connie never slowed, heading for the door in question. 'Pete' had an extra helping of stupid that morning with his breakfast I guess because he grabbed her by the arm.

"You can't leave, Doctor-" and that was as far as he got before I clocked him in the jaw. I was moving when I hit him so my weight was behind it and he staggered back two steps before sprawling on the floor, tripped up by his chair.

"Go!" I said urgently and pushed her toward the door as I shoved Baby's keys into her hand. She never hesitated. 'Pete' and his aborted attempt to stop us from leaving was all the proof we needed that things had gotten real in a hurry. 'Pete' was trying to get up.

"Do yourself a favor and stay there," I warned. "You should never have put your hands on her. Do it again and I'll end you." I shouldn't have said that I guess, but I was mad. What I really wanted to do was put a round in his head but I figured he was following orders. Of course he had to be the type that would attack a woman to get those orders and follow them, but still he was just a peon. That witch Madeline was responsible for this.

There was no way any of this shit was legal and that was all the justification I needed for anything I had to do to keep us from being trapped in that hospital. I was out the door right behind Connie. She was already inside, driver's door open. I flipped the kill switch as I climbed in and hit the key. Baby started right up and five seconds later we were moving.

"Buckle up," I ordered, doing the same as I negotiated the parking lot. "I expect things to be exciting on the trip home."

"I can't believe she would try that shit!" Connie was angry now that the immediate danger was past. "After all we did today!"

"She needs a bullet in the head," I nodded. At this point I probably should have been alarmed at how easy it was becoming for me to think about using violence on people. I wasn't though. Everyone I'd done anything to had been asking for it. I hadn't really had anything to do with Vaccine Guy and Towel Girl (never did get their names. Sorry.), but I had killed Methie of course, threatened a soldier, punched out the janitorial guy at the back door, the list was growing.

This was what I had been worrying over, to be honest. Things were getting really bad and people like Madeline were trying to force others into a bad situation to cover their asses. She and others like her still hadn't gotten it yet. Ass covering days were coming to an end. Her court order or whatever it was wouldn't be worth the paper it was written on without someone who had the ability to enforce it. Jacobs might or might not do it, but there would be someone, somewhere, who would.

And sooner or later I'd probably have to kill them.

"Watch behind us," I ordered. "Make sure no one gets on our tail. And help me watch for trouble," I added.

"It's dark," she noted.

"That happens when the sun goes down," I nodded absently.

"Smart ass," she shot back. "I meant it's *dark*. A lot of the lights are out."

I had not noticed that so intent was I on escaping our almost prison, but she was right. About half the street lights were off, usually in strips of five or six. Almost like every other circuit was off or blown.

"I didn't mean it smart," I told her. "I've been thinking about the sun being down when you would be out for a while now. Freaks come out at night," I added, remembering an old song from my childhood.

"Too true," she nodded as she turned to look behind us. "I don't think anyone is following us. Not that I can tell, anyway."

"Keep an eye out," I replied. "I'll change us up some as we go, take some wrong streets, that kind of thing. That should help us see if there's someone following us."

I proceeded to do just that, weaving through traffic and turning quickly at odd places to see if anyone pursued.

"Nothing," Connie reported after the third such turn. "I think we're okay."

"Then let's get home," I said, pulling out onto the highway and gunning the engine.

"Let's do," she sighed.

CHAPTER FOURTEEN

Okay, so *saying* 'Lets get home' is far easier than actually *doing* it sometimes. As we hit the main flow of traffic it became apparent that Madeline was not the only one trying to exert her influence on others. We could see roving groups of people that ranged from obvious gangs to collections of business owners to what looked to be more or less neighborhood watch patrols. The lights being off in places allowed the shine from a half dozen fires to glow against the night sky, giving the town a spooky look. Like something from a scary movie.

I didn't want to be in a scary movie. Or any movie for that matter.

Worse, I had not really taken into account how noticeable Big Baby was. I mean I never had worried about it since I always enjoyed showing her off, you know? What had always seemed to be a plus for all that hard work was now looking like an impediment.

"You know it's going to be hard to hide in this thing," Connie said just then, almost as if reading my mind.

"I'd just thought of that," I admitted. "Taking this thing seemed the way to go this morning. I thought we might need the power or the height to get around. You know? Now she's just a shining beacon telling everyone where we are."

"They would know anyway," Connie pointed out. "I was actually thinking that it would be hard to get around without drawing attention we might not want. We're obviously better prepared than, well, everybody," she raised her hands in a shrug. "Panicky people tend to try and attach themselves to someone who can protect them. We look like that someone."

She was right. Another thing I hadn't thought of, not really. Sure I went through that brief bit where I thought about James maybe wanting to impose on my non-existent hospitality, but otherwise I hadn't considered it. I mean, not many people knew I was into preparedness at all, so it never crossed my mind to be overly concerned about others wanting to make themselves at home on my dime.

Don't misunderstand me now. I got nothing against helping others where I can. But this wasn't shaping up to be one of those times. It was looking like a complete and total breakdown in society, followed of course by the potential for hordes of the walking dead dining on anyone they happen to catch up with.

At a time like that, I admit that helping others took a back seat to helping myself. Sounds bad maybe, but I prefer pragmatic. Doesn't do me any good to help someone at my own expense. We just both end up dead.

"You have an excellent point," I sighed. "I hadn't considered it that way either. I'm used to hiding. Well, mostly," I added. "Lot of people know I'm a shooter, or a hunter, or a prepper, but not all three. In fact only you really knew all that," I admitted. "Moment of weakness for a pretty girl who happened to be a kindred spirit," I grinned.

"Sure," she rolled her eyes as she drew the word out. "So what do we do?" she asked.

"We go home," I repeated. "Like I said, that was the rationale behind using this beast to start with. So we could get home, no matter what. If someone tries to stop us or follow us, we deal with it as it comes. There's really nothing else to do. But we are done venturing out into the world after this," I told her. "No more. We've helped as many people as we can. We've done more than most and that's enough. It's seriously time we start looking after ourselves. Past it, really."

"Okay," she nodded. "All helping others has done is cause us more trouble."

"Too true," I had to agree. "Okay, we're almost to the bridge," I noted. "Are we still looking okay?" I had no sooner than spoke when a set of headlights came bouncing out of a side street and onto the road behind us. I tensed, wondering if this was going to be a police car. I didn't want to shoot a cop but if he tried to stop us or take Connie back to that hospital then whatever happened to him was his fault I reasoned.

"Is that a cop, you think?" I asked her, unable to look away from the crazy traffic for long. "And are they *following* us, or just behind us?"

"Lights are too bright, I can't make it out," Connie admitted, turning in her seat to look between us. "Wait." I waited but there was nothing else.

"How long do I wait?" I asked.

"It's a truck," she said finally. "A low-rider from the look of it. That's why it looked like a car."

"That could be good or bad," I mused. "Good that it's not a cop sent to try and drag you back to the hospital-"

"Try?" she interrupted.

"Yeah that's not happening," I assured her. "Or bad that it's someone who was waiting for someone like us who, as you pointed out, looks prepared."

"Or it could just be someone who's in a hurry to get somewhere," she added.

"That too," I agreed. "Anything else? If it was a medical emergency they'd be going the other way."

"True," she mused. "Could be going to help a family member in trouble, or trying to get someplace they created with just this scenario in mind."

"You mean an emergency in general or the Zombie Apocalypse?" I had to ask. "Cause if they anticipated the Zombie Apocalypse that doesn't seem to speak highly of their mental state."

"Unless you're having a Zombie Apocalypse," she pointed out wryly.

"Another good point," I conceded. "What are they doing?" I asked as the lights behind us moved across my mirror.

"They're coming up beside us," she warned, turning back in her seat and drawing her pistol. She held it in both hands, down between her knees.

"Hold on," I ordered and hit the brakes. I didn't slam them on like in the movies since that's an extremely dumb thing to do (*especially* in a high profile vehicle) but I didn't just tap them like you would to get a tailgater to back off of your bumper, either. One of the upgrades I had made on Baby was an anti-lock brake system. It hadn't been cheap, but like I said; brakes locking on a ride this tall is a bad move.

Baby's speed dropped off in a hurry and the accelerating low rider raced by us. Now we would see what happened. I hit the gas again but not nearly as hard, waiting.

The low-rider's brake lights came on.

"Well, I guess that answers that question," I sighed, downshifting manually and hitting the gas again. The truck looked as if it was going to try and cut us off and I timed it just right, hitting the left lane just as he hit ours, flooring the accelerator at the same time. Four hundred and fifty horses screamed beneath the hood as Big Baby shot past the truck, accelerating rapidly as we did so. As we shot by I caught a glimpse of a shotgun barrel in the driver's window.

"Gun!" I shouted, but Connie had already seen it. We were by before the shotgun could be used on us, but now it was behind us. I began to weave from one lane to the other hoping it would make us harder to hit. I already knew that there was no way for us to outrun this guy. His truck wasn't pushing nearly as much weight or rubber as Big Baby was and might have almost as much horsepower. We were going to have to try something different.

Connie reached across to the console and hit the switch for the rear window.

"What are you doing?" I asked her. Riding with the rear window open on one of these things was a first class invite to carbon monoxide poisoning.

"I can't stand someone on my ass," she almost snarled and I very diplomatically didn't make the smart ass remark that came to me in a flash of male genius. She unbuckled her seat belt and turned in her seat.

"Are you goi-" My voice was drowned out and my night vision ruined for a few seconds by the flash of Connie ripping off three shots out the back window.

According to what she told me, since I couldn't see it myself, the low rider's windshield starred nicely and most likely scared the absolute shit out of the driver. The truck swerved sharply as the driver apparently slammed on his brakes. He had apparently not opted for the anti-locking upgrade because the truck wobbled twice, left to right, before sliding around sideways in the road and coming to a stop even as we roared away. Thankfully we had managed to outrun most of the other traffic so there was no one else close enough to hit the idiot. Connie turned around cool as a cucumber to roll the window back up and then refasten her seat belt.

"Nice." That was all I had. Just could not think of anything else. Inappropriate or otherwise.

"Thanks," she nodded, still just as cool as you please. If I hadn't already been in love with her, that would have done it right there.

Fifteen minutes later we pulled into the house with no further signs of trouble. Twenty minutes and Baby was hidden around back and we were inside behind locked gates and barred doors.

Thirty minutes and we were conserving water. Think about it, it'll come to you.

*****

Connie dropped onto the sofa beside me still toweling her hair dry. She'd put on a pair of those wonderful boy shorts and a tank-top. I was wearing gym shorts and a tee while I surfed the news channels. My computer was open on the coffee table in front of me and a hand held scanner sitting next to it.

"So what's the word?" she asked.

"Nothing on the scanner about the 'incident'," I told her. "Probably didn't want to risk the report."

"I wonder if they got our tag number?" she mused. "They might be able to use it to track us."

"Would if it was the right tag," I nodded absently. "It's registered to an undercover cop car. They run that tag and they got more trouble than a shot out windshield."

"How did you get something like that?" Connie was astonished.

"Stole it," I admitted easily. "It was out-of-date anyway," I shrugged. "I keep tags on

363

an old junker car to keep the stickers up to date. Never know when it might come in handy. I put it on before we left for the hospital this morning, just in case."

"You are just full of surprises Mister Drake," she shook her head as she curled up next to me. "So what else is going on?"

"Guard is out across the country," I told her. "They're considering using the active military now for manpower but there's a political battle going on over all that."

"What are they arguing about?" Connie was astonished.

"*Posse Comitatus*, believe it or not," I told her. "It's amazing how little sense our elected officials actually have even in times like these."

"You expected better?" she asked.

"No, not really. I did expect they'd all be in a bunker somewhere by now, citing the 'continuation of government' or whatever that phrase is."

"Continuity," she chuckled dryly. "The word you're looking for is continuity."

"Yeah, that," I agreed. "Anyway, the city is burning," I got to the local stuff. "Turns out some of the glow we were seeing was coming from there, no just on the far side of town. Whole blocks are going up and there's not enough firemen to contain it. And that was before so many decided to abandon ship."

"You blame them?" she asked me, leaning her head against my arm.

"Hell no," I shook my head, raising my arm to wrap around her shoulders. "I would have been long gone myself already. This whole thing has been handled wrong from the start," I added. "You can't tell me this couldn't have been contained. It would have taken some hard choices I don't deny, but it could have been done."

"Take more courage than that outfit has," Connie replied.

"They were probably too busy jockeying for position to worry about it," I agreed. "Now it's probably too late."

"Not certainly?" she asked, head raising to look at me.

"There's probably still time to get this under control," I replied. "It will take someone with enough balls to make that decision though. And there is not a Napoleon among them," I quoted from an old civil war story I'd read once about Shiloh.

"What's that mean?" she asked.

"It means that there's a clear path to follow, but no one to lead them down it," I shrugged again. "There's only one way to stop this and that's to head shot every infected. Do it now, tonight, while you can. While you've still got the structure and the logistics to get the job done. Another day, two at most, and you won't have it. You're losing people every minute and some of them will be the people you're depending on. Just that simple."

"Once you reach a point where everyone sees that we can't win, they cut their losses and hunker down to take care of themselves and their families. In some places it's already too late."

"Like us?" she asked wryly, eyebrows raised.

"We're not soldiers, police, any of the emergency services personnel they need for this," I shook my head. "We're actually doing the smart, best thing for them by staying the hell outta their way," I pointed out. "Well meaning amateurs getting in the way just makes things worse. And it's definitely bad enough as it is."

"Point," she nodded. "Hungry?" she asked.

"I could eat," I admitted, cursing mentally at the abandoned Double Big Jack sitting in the doctor's office of the ER. That right there was grounds enough to shoot that bitch Madeline if I ever saw her again. Probably the last one I would ever get, too.

"Keep an eye on things while I fix us a sandwich," she said, getting to her feet. Before she could move her cell phone rang. We both looked at it with no small trepidation as she reached for it. The number was from the hospital.

"What do you think?" she asked.

"Is it her number?" I asked.

"No, but that doesn't mean anything," she admitted.

"Anyone else there you'd want to talk to?" I checked.

"Well, no."

"Turn it off," I told her. "Forget it." She nodded and powered the phone down, setting it back on the coffee table.

"One *healthy* sandwich coming up," she taunted me, but I just nodded.

"Makes sense after all that junk food," I admitted. Didn't get the lion-killer smile for that, but it was a smile none-the-less.

I'd take it.

I watched as the news kept playing over the places where things had gone from bad to horrible over the course of the day. There were a *lot* of them, too. It just didn't seem like all this could have happened in two days or so, which led me to think that it hadn't. This shit had already been here in the states when Dumbo had gone on television saying that it wasn't and that precautions were being taken and all that other bureaucratic horseshit they shovel the public when they don't want to admit to something.

I realized right then that the worst thing that could happen would be if the zombies *didn't* eat all politicians, everywhere. As long as they got them, then maybe those of us who survived would be okay. *Maybe.*

Connie returned with a pair of sandwiches, some baked chips and a soda apiece, probably an apology for the healthy food she was forcing on me. I didn't mind really. I needed to be be healthy now.

"I have to keep you healthy," she jibed, smiling at me. Again it was like she could read my mind. "Despite your obvious failings I want to keep you around," she added.

"Love me too much to lose me, huh?" I shot back, taking a huge bite of a corned beef on rye.

"Yes." It was a simple word, yes, yet it carried so much with it. I paused in my chewing, regretting the enormous bite I had taken since my mouth was full. I carefully looked her way to see her studying me carefully.

"Yes," she said again, nodding this time.

I finally managed to swallow though it took some work. She hadn't really said it back to me at the hospital and I had almost forgotten it, what with the shooting, the assault and battery, the near incarceration at the hospital of doom, you know, all that.

"Ah," I started, but then stopped, not really knowing what to say. She smirked slightly and took a bite of her own sandwich, removing the need for me to say anything. I just smiled a little and kept eating. Side by side with the woman of my dreams who had just told me she loved me. All while the world was falling apart around us. What was there to add to that, really?

So we sat there eating healthy and watching the world slowly fall apart as each and every bite from an infected became another enemy. Another problem.

We watched long into the night, getting up every now and then to check things, use the bathroom, refill water glasses, the usual stuff you do when watching the end of the world with loved ones.

Because at the moment that was all we *could* do. Sit and wait and watch.

*****

Early Wednesday morning, two days after the hospital debacle, we got a rather rude reminder that things truly can 'always be worse'. It was something I should have thought of but didn't. I can't say why, exactly. I'm not making excuses, I should have thought of it. It just didn't occur to me for this particular situation.

And no one wants to think about nuclear weapons.

The Chinese had apparently had it pretty bad. No way of knowing how bad since they closed themselves off when things got bad. But it must have been *really* bad (wow, that's a lot of bads) there since they lit off three tactical nukes on their own soil. Beijing, Shanghai, Hong-Kong. No warning, no notice to other nations, nothing. Just three explosions that registered on the Richter scale and were visible from space.

Seeing the images from the ISS made me think of something else. What would the astros on the station do now? Safe to say no one was really concerned with resupplying five guys and a woman who were a long way from home while hundreds of thousands were dead, dying, or undead. Honestly, by that time the casualties were probably in the millions. There's just no way to know since all the governments were lying their asses off about the whole thing until it was too late to do anything about it. That had always seemed like just an inconvenience before.

This time it might have caused the end of mankind.

I know, I know, drama and all that. Doesn't make it any less true. Their poor decision making (stupidity) coupled with their inability to make hard choices (cowardice) and some extremely *poor* leadership skills by people in extremely *important* leadership positions had left us, by which I mean the *world*, in a pretty tough situation. By the time those that were left admitted there was a 'problem', it was a whole hell of a lot worse than 'problem'. Problem is a math word. That's what one of my old professors had said anyway. Well, here's some math for you.

Seven *billion* (that's with a B) people, all of whom were potential zombies. One bite, which is all it takes to infect someone (seen that for myself). Every infected had the absolute potential, almost guaranteed in the early days, of infecting at least one other person before being 'contained' (an insurance term if ever I heard one). The math said that this was a 'problem' that had the potential to grow exponentially. You know, one makes two, two makes four, four makes eight and so on until we reached that tipping point where the infected outnumber the uninfected.

Consider this; one thousand infected in a city of five million people is something like point zero one percent of the population. Manageable, right? I mean the average redneck (I can say that since I are one) has enough ammunition for his handy deer rifle to take care of twenty or so, no problem. This is a problem that any well trained and equipped metropolitan police force could handle alone, let alone with the assistance of the National Guard.

There's where the trouble starts. No one in a position of authority was willing to give those kind of orders. I know in hindsight it's easy to make that judgment, but bear with me. The initial stages of the infection, when no one realized what was happening or what it might mean, you wouldn't even consider euthanasia of the infected. No civilized society would make such a leap before ensuring that the infected had no hope of recovery and that the problem would continue to spread like wildfire until it was eliminated. I would not have advocated for something like that at the start and would have probably screamed bloody murder if anyone else had.

But once that video from Spain had been released, certainly by the time the video from Germany had hit the net, added to the discovery that there was no cure, that the infected were in fact now medically dead, or undead maybe, at that point some tough decisions are in order.

If they're medically dead, or undead, then there's no hope of recovery. No cure or antidote is going to fix this problem. You can't cure *dead*.

Now, I'm not saying it would have been an easy decision. I am saying that the decision should have been made. For my way of thinking, once I know there's no help for the infected, no way to restore them or 'cure' them, then the focus has to be on stopping the spread of the infection. You do that by stopping the infected.

Had that line been adopted after those facts had been established, then the average community, at least here in America, was more than capable of defending itself from the dead. Or *un*dead. Whatever.

See what I mean? We could have stopped this before it got so out of hand that China felt the need to nuke three of it's major cities. To tell the truth, now that I put all of this in writing, I'm surprised that China of all places couldn't get a handle on the situation. Everything I've ever read about the Chinese government and their philosophies leaves me with the impression that individual rights simply don't compute with them. With communism in general in fact. It's all about the 'collective'. If that's really accurate, then you would think that the Chinese would be the first government to embrace the idea of eliminating the infected so as to protect the rest of us. All I can figure is that the problem was out of control before they realized it.

And thus we awaken to find that at midnight our time, which was noon their time give or take (I think), China had nuked the three worse infestations in their nation. 'Demands' from other nations to pledge they would not do so again apparently fell on deaf, or maybe undead, ears.

We know all this because the news people were still on the job. Several of them, like Kelly Amberly, (or was it Amberyly Kelly? I can't remember and it's not worth looking back to check) had been eaten in the field, but despite that they were still on the job. I have to admit that made me rethink some harsh things I'd said in the past about reporters in general. Not the talking heads that sat behind a desk and 'reported' on someone else's hard work. They were still jerks. But the people in the field, they were sticking. Reporting any and everything they could find out for as long as they could.

Because of them and the work they did, there are a lot of people alive today who were able to stay that way because they knew what was going on, where it was happening and how bad things were. They knew where to avoid, who to avoid and what to do to prepare for trouble in their area. And thanks to them they knew when trouble had arrived in their area too.

I have to pause here for a minute and remember the people who were not professional reporters, but were still using social media and other means to get local news out to anyone who still had access to that media. Local reports in many cases came from these amateur news seekers who were trying to fill the void and provide information to their local area. Again, there are a lot of people alive today that wouldn't be if not for them. And a lot of them didn't make it.

It was in fact because of these folks who were still out there trying to report on the event that we heard the first good news we had received since all this had started. Something that made me think there just might still be a chance at least some of us to survive, maybe even see a day when we might see things return to whatever 'normal' we could salvage in a post zombie apocalypse society.

*****

At some point an Army Colonel realized that sending his men into action without permission to fire was just adding to the ranks of the undead. You send soldiers to fight but don't allow them to fight and you lose them to the infection. This man was not willing to sacrifice his men like that and ordered them to open fire on anyone that was infected.

Believe it or not there was a modest uproar about that. Modest because most of the idiots that were 'advocating for the infected', (that's really what they called it.

You can't make this shit up), had been eaten by the infected or else had joined them. Still, those few talking heads that remained went on the airwaves that were still operating and demanded that the soldiers be ordered to use non-lethal force only and that the Colonel and any of his men who had shot 'innocent victims of the plague' (seriously. *Cannot*. Make. This. Up.) be tried for murder.

There was of course no talk of them going to assist with all that. 'Not my place', etc and so on. Nor was there any talk of the 'innocent victims' being held responsible for their crimes since clearly they were beyond reason.

How's that for idiot logic. Idiology? No, that would be the study of idiots, wouldn't it. Anyway. We can't use deadly force to deal with homicidal 'innocent victims' who are killing random people left and right everywhere you look because they had rights.

News Flash Number One: They're *dead*. No rights.

News Flash Number Two: *We're* still alive. *We* have rights. Or, if you insist, we have rights, *too*. Either way, we had the absolute right of self-defense. And apparently this Army guy decided that extended to him and his men. Which it absolutely should have from the very beginning.

So he and his men began to eradicate the zombies wherever they found them. Anyone bitten but not 'turned' was locked up to see what happened. Honestly I'm pretty sure they were hoping someone wouldn't turn, thinking that might be the key to unlock the door to a vaccine or antidote. I mean, you know, one you could take before you turned. Or whatever.

It was a relief of sorts to see that at least some of the news people still on the air were supportive of the Colonel, and cheered him on. These were some of the same people who had watched friends and colleagues eaten on live television so they were probably a little biased at this point, but as far as I was concerned their bias was well placed.

All it took was one man to stand up to the insanity of those stupid orders for others to follow. As word of what Colonel Guy, (that was his name, Guy. Like the Raider's Punter? The one the collegiate punter award is named after. I think? You don't care about that and there's no football these days anyway). So anyway. As word of what Guy had done spread, other military commanders began to issue similar orders followed by several large police departments. Almost all large city agencies had lost manpower to the infected so for them it probably came easy for those left to start putting the infected down.

For the rest of the day the remaining newsies were alternately livid about what was happening, disgruntled that it hadn't happened sooner, or tickled shitless over the whole thing and cheering the soldiers on as they cleared area after area of the undead.

Connie and I watched from the house, me taking an occasional stroll around the property checking the fence and what have you and Connie pouring over the internet for anything we could use information wise.

Turned out Connie had done a lot of infectious work when she was with Doctors Without Borders. Not her specialty, as she was what she called a 'general internist (I still don't know what that means). As my grandfather had put it once, 'she can't play the tune but she can dance to it'. She knew enough to get by, and maybe to be helpful if there ever came a time when there was a chance in hell of making headway against it.

But that time was not now. I admit it, there was some selfishness involved in my argument. I didn't want anything to happen to her. But there was another fact as well. When this was over, *if* it was over, then doctors might well be in short supply. And they would be sorely needed if the chance to rebuild presented itself. Our own experience in a small town hospital was enough to show me that medical personnel had likely suffered disproportionate casualties as they saw infected in the emergency rooms across the country. Across the world for that matter.

If things ever 'straightened out', so to speak, then she would be needed like never before. She and every other doctor left alive, along with every nurse, every medical specialist, every paramedic, police officer, firefighter, engineer, you name the profession and it was probably going to play a huge part in our being able to rebuild our world and start over.

But we had to survive first.

*****

And so here we sit. It's been five days since our trip home from the hospital. Of course we've found holes in our preps since then. Bound to happen, but it's still annoying. We could take a chance on going to find what we need but we can see from the net cams in town that the zombie issue is alive and well in our little slice of heaven.

I've killed two 'walkers', as people have taken to calling them, when they approached the fence. I didn't know them, for which I am grateful. I'm going to have to get rid of them I guess but I'm reluctant to go outside. I saw a coyote tearing at one late yesterday and wondered idly if the coyote could be zombiefied. Would that not be some shit right there?

An undead coyote. Of course that would mean we might see undead bears, wolves, mountain lions . . . an image of an undead, zombified Bigfoot just popped into my head. Did not need that. Just did not need it.

So we're settled in trying to wait for the end of the world, or at least to the end of the Zombies. No idea which will come first, though I'm fairly certain that zombies everywhere will count toward the end of the world. It should, anyway. I'm positive that if I see a zombie Bigfoot that we're doomed. Just doomed.

We're set pretty well except for water and there's been rain all day today so the water situation should be okay for a while. We're set for food of course and most everything else we can think of. Phone service has become spotty but it's still working in fits and starts.

FRIGGIN' ZOMBIES

Three of five local television stations are still on the air. Fox and CNN are still there but MSNBC folded yesterday, citing the 'danger to their employees' as the reason they closed down. Fox and CNN faced the same threats but over a dozen of their people at each HQ volunteered to stay there and on the air as long as they could. Brave folks like I said before.

Stupid. But brave. They aren't getting much new information really. Mostly they're mapping out places they have lost contact with. There's a lot of them. The little 'new' news is from people like Colonel Guy as he and his men fight to clear at least some safe zone and keep it that way. His projected safe zone is about two hundred miles from us, give or take. I admit I've been studying a map of the area between here and where he is. You know, just for reference.

Live cams that are still streaming over the net let us see zombies showing up all over now. Doesn't seem possible that all this happened so fast but. . .well, there it is. Now it's a race to see if adopting the 'eradicate' policy will still work, considering the ZA was already well and truly underway before they started trying to do that. All we can do is hunker down and wait it out. Wait to see if Colonel Guy can make his 'safe zone' happen. Wait and see if he and his men and the few others that have adopted the same policy can prevail or not. There's no 'Guy' in our area, hence the map study.

Just in case.

Hardly seems like it's only be a few days since I saw that video on the net. Lot has happened since then. Managed to get most everything I could need to have in order to survive, assuming we can keep disaster to a minimum and it rains regular. Even got the girl. And ain't that some shit right there?

Finally get my dream girl and BOOM. . .zombies. Or maybe it was zombies and THEN I got the girl. I'm gonna have to get back to ya on that one. Either way though, who'd of thought it? Friggin' zombies, man.

Go figure.

THE END

THANK YOU FOR READING

"FRIGGIN ZOMBIES"

ENJOY THIS BOOK?

CHECK OUT THESE OTHER GREAT TITLES

by

N.C. REED!

Parno's Company
Tammy and Ringo
Roland
Odd Billy Todd
The Monster of Creasy's Hollow

ALSO VISIT OUR WEBSITE
At
www.creativetexts.com

THANK YOU!

www.ingramcontent.com/pod-product-compliance
Lightning Source LLC
Chambersburg PA
CBHW050613110726
47899CB00001B/91